HAMSTER-SAURUS ReX

BY TOM O'DONNELL
ILLUSTRATIONS BY TIM MILLER

HAMS SAU R

TER-
RUS-
eX

HARPER
An Imprint of HarperCollins Publishers

CONTENTS

CERTAIN CLASS PETS will go down in legend. We've all heard of the duck from Marneyville Elementary that could use an electric pencil sharpener. And of course there was Bert, the chameleon that Ms. Simonson's fourth graders all swore they saw go plaid that one time. Some kids at my cousin's school still whisper of a goldfish that could see fifteen minutes into the future but was cursed with the inability to tell anyone what it had learned. Because, you know, it was a goldfish.

Impressive as these creatures are, none of them can compare to Hamstersaurus Rex. He was a giant among rodents, a folk hero for all time. He was the pride of Mr. Copeland's sixth-grade class. Most of all, he was my friend.

Nobody knew where Hammie Rex came from. All we knew is that when we returned to school after Columbus Day, there was a hamster cage in the corner. Mr. Copeland seemed as surprised as anybody.

"Well, kids, I guess we have a hamster now," he said with a shrug. "Nobody at this school ever tells me anything."

"I wish this hamster was a turtle," said Tina Gomez. "Do you think the pet shop has an exchange policy?"

"I bet we could return him and get, like, a hundred and fifty snails," said Wilbur Weber. Wilbur had a lot of snails at home. I guess it wasn't enough.

I looked into the cage. At first glance he appeared to be a normal hamster:

orange fur, pink nose, beady black eyes. Then he opened his mouth and made a weird growling noise. The other kids were startled. Even though he was the size of a muffin, this hamster wasn't afraid of anything.

"I think the new hamster's cool," I said, drawing a quick sketch of the little guy in my notebook.

"Nah, I think it's dumb," said Beefer Vanderkoff, squinting at me from across the room. His real name is Kiefer, but only teachers call him that.

"Stow it, Beefer," said Dylan D'Amato. She's my best friend, also pretty fearless.

"Kids, enough," said Mr. Copeland, frowning.

Martha Cherie raised her hand. "Um, Arnold, may I address the class, please?" she said. Everyone but Beefer rolled their eyes.

"Okay, Martha," said Mr. Copeland. "But seriously, you have to call me 'Mr. Copeland,' okay? We've been over this."

She nodded and turned to face the rest of us. "Classmates, I just wanted to tell you that even though having a pet seems like it's all fun and games, in reality it's a huge responsibility that you're probably not ready for."

"Um, why?" asked Dylan. Martha Cherie rubbed her the wrong way like no one else.

"Because, Dylan, most of you are careless and, quite frankly, immature. I took an online quiz, and it said my mental age is forty-five, so . . ."

"Caring for a hamster isn't rocket science," said Dylan. "You give it food and water every day and change the wood chips once a week. I think we can handle it."

"Well, my uncle Tony happens to be a zoologist who specializes in hamsters, and he says it's much, *much* more complicated than that," said Martha with a smug look on her face. "I just think it would be for the best if we were to pick someone—a person known for being very, *very* responsible—and assigned her the duty of caring for our beloved new class pet."

Mr. Copeland sighed. "Yes, fine, Martha, you can be Hamster Monitor."

She squealed with glee, an incredibly disturbing sound. "Oh thank you ever so much, Arn— Er, I mean Mr. Copeland. May I ask: Will I be issued an official Hamster Monitor ID card and lanyard?"

"No," said Mr. Copeland.

"I'll make my own," said Martha.

"Knock yourself out," said Mr. Copeland. "Okay. So who's ready to learn about Pilgrims?"

"Excuse me, Mr. Copeland." Martha had her hand up again.

Mr. Copeland rubbed his temples. "Yes, Martha."

"I think the new hamster should have a name."

"Fine."

"As Hamster Monitor, I officially decree that the hamster's name is Toothbrush."

This prompted a chorus of boos from the other kids.

"No, no, no," said Caroline Moody. "Let's call him Xullthrox the Destroyer."

More boos.

"What about Shelly?" said Wilbur Weber.

Still more boos. Maybe Wilbur could only think up good names for snails?

"I think the hamster should be called Martha Junior," said Beefer. The boos stopped. Everyone stared at him in silence. "I mean, I don't know. Whatever," he said. "Man, everybody shut up."

Suddenly, the perfect name came to me in a flash. I didn't dare speak up again for fear of provoking Beefer further. Instead, I wrote it on a scrap of paper and passed it to Dylan while Mr. Copeland wasn't looking.

Dylan read the note and nodded, satisfied. "Look, we're calling the little dude Hamstersaurus Rex," she said to the class. "End of discussion."

They all stared at her now. Coming from me, the name would have been a hard sell. But most people actually liked Dylan.

"Just look at his tiny little T. rex arms," Dylan added with a shrug, like it was obvious.

The class did look. Everyone agreed that his arms were indeed very tiny.

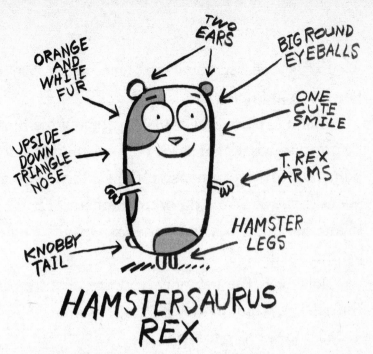

HAMSTERSAURUS REX

"I don't know, Dylan," said Tina. "I guess I see the arms thing. But how else is he like a dinosaur? He doesn't—"

The hamster growled again.

That settled it. The sixth-grade class hamster was officially Hamstersaurus Rex. Everybody seemed happy about it except Beefer. He must have been pretty attached to the name Martha Junior.

"Now about those Pilgrims," said Mr. Copeland. "So, way back in the sixteen hundreds everybody wore these funny hats—"

"Excuse me, Mr. Copeland." Once again, Martha had her hand up.

"Martha," said Mr. Copeland, gritting his teeth. "We've already spent a lot of time talking about hamsters this morning, so if the sentence you are about to say contains the word 'hamster,' I'm going to ask you not to say the sentence. Okay?"

She nodded.

"Now, *does* the sentence you are about to say contain the word 'hamster'?"

Martha shook her head.

"Okay, then," said Mr. Copeland. "What is it?"

"As official monitor of a *specific type of rodent*, I just wanted to tell you that *specific type of rodent* is gone."

"What?" said Mr. Copeland.

"Just look," said Martha. She pointed to the cage. Sure enough, it was empty. The little door swung open on its hinges.

"Well, kids," said Mr. Copeland, scratching his head. "I guess we don't have a hamster anymore."

MISSING!
HAVE YOU SEEN THIS HAMSTER?

Last seen in Mr. Copeland's Room. If you have any information report immediately to Sam Gibbs

CHAPTER 2

NOBODY SAW HAMSTERSAURUS REX for a week after that. Most of the other kids seemed to forget about him. Not Martha Cherie, though. She never stopped wearing her home-made Hamster Monitor ID lanyard.

I didn't forget, either. Before school, I poked around our classroom looking for any sign of him. I searched the halls between classes. I asked kids from other grades if they'd seen him. I even put up missing hamster posters—hand-drawn by yours truly. Still nothing. Dylan thought I was nuts, but I never lost hope that he would one day return. Even though I'd known him for all of four minutes, I couldn't help it; I liked the little guy.

It was Tuesday, after school, when I made a terrible mistake. While checking to see if Hamstersaurus Rex was hiding in the faucet of one of the sinks in the second-floor boys' bathroom, I accidentally sprayed water everywhere. Well, not everywhere, exactly. Most of it went right onto Beefer Vanderkoff's T-shirt.

"Arrgh!" growled Beefer. "You got my shirt all wet, dummy!"

"Beefer! I didn't see you there. Here, let me get that for you," I said, grabbing a paper towel to dab the shirt, which had a picture of a zombie throwing up on it. "If it's any consolation, I'm pretty sure water doesn't stain."

"Is that some kind of a joke?" said Beefer, squinting at me. "You know I'm a clear belt in karate, don't you?"

"Clear belt?" I said.

"Yup. It's one level above a black belt," said Beefer. "It's so hard to get that nobody even knows about it. The final test is, they make you head-butt a rock in half."

"Hey, that's great," I said. "Congratulations on your clear belt. Yay, Beefer!" I won't sugarcoat it—I was groveling.

Beefer scowled. "Is that sarcasm? You think you're so funny, with your funny little pictures. Man, you wouldn't last one minute down at the dojo. You know what would happen?"

"Uh, what?"

"This: *Keeeee-yah!*" Beefer shrieked, and punched the trash can. It wobbled for a second and then fell over, spilling a pile of wet paper towels onto the floor.

"Wait . . . ," I said, genuinely confused. "I'm the trash can in that scenario? Or the guy fighting it?"

"Shut up," hissed Beefer, clutching his knuckles and gritting his teeth in pain. Someone like you or me might have guessed that punching a metal object would hurt your hand. Beefer had to figure these things out for himself.

"I can't believe you forced me to use my karate in anger," he said, as he winced and flexed his fingers. "I'm going to kill you for that."

That was my cue. I dashed past him through the door and out into the hallway.

"Get back here, Sam!" yelled Beefer behind me.

I ran for my life.

You have to understand: running for my life isn't my favorite activity in the world. In fact,

running for any reason is pretty low on the list. I enjoy reading comic books. Playing disc golf with Dylan is fun (even though I never win). Occasionally, I like to put a second pair of shoes on my hands and pretend I'm a horse. (Actually, maybe don't tell anybody about that last one.) These days, though, running for my life seemed to take up an awful lot of my free time. Thanks to Beefer, it was my number one forced hobby.

It all went back to my *actual* favorite activity in the world: drawing. I love to draw stuff. Always have. Other kids used to think it was cool, almost like a magic trick. That changed last year.

I'd just mastered drawing robots punching each other's heads off, and I wanted to work on my caricature skills. For practice, I drew a caricature

of every single kid in our class. I wasn't going to show them to anybody. (Okay, I showed them to Dylan. She laughed at hers.) But one day I accidentally left my sketchbook in the library. Caroline Moody found it, and soon *everyone* had seen their official Sam Gibbs portrait. They were all pretty mad—except Martha Cherie, who was eerily flattered. Angriest of all was Beefer Vanderkoff. I'll admit the stink lines around his head may have crossed a line.

I still wasn't exactly popular with the other kids, but only Beefer wanted to flatten me. As far as I could tell, flattening people was one of three things he actually cared about—along with horror movies and processed food. Without a zombie DVD or a package of Funchos Southwest-Style Teriyaki-Ranch Flavor-Wedges (A SmilesCorp Product™) to distract him, I was in serious trouble.

"I'm going to hit you so hard that you forget how to do long division," he yelled as he chased me. "Seriously, this beating is going to affect your report card!"

I had only one hope: Beefer probably wouldn't

pummel me in front of Mr. Copeland. I ran toward our classroom. As I skidded around a corner, my heart sank. The lights were off. The room was empty. Mr. Copeland had already gone home for the day. That meant the door would be locked. In desperation, I tried anyway.

Success! The knob turned. I ducked inside, closed the door, and locked it behind me. Then I got down on all fours and hid behind a row of desks. I won't sugarcoat it: I was cowering.

I could hear Beefer outside now, right outside the door.

"Where are you, Sam?" he yelled. "Seriously, you better not be reading my diary. There's personal stuff in— I mean, I don't keep a diary. Shut up!"

He tried the knob. It turned, and I heard the door swing open. I buried my face in my palm. Of course Mr. Copeland *had* locked the door before he left. It was just that the lock was broken! Beefer stepped inside.

"You're in here somewhere, Sam," he said. "Believe me, I've had enough detentions to know every single inch of this classroom. You can't hide from me. I'll find you. I'm like a modern-day Sunblock Holmes."

Silently I crawled along the row of desks. Things were getting desperate now. I looked around for something, anything, that might save me.

Graphing calculator? Nope.

Tube of puff paint? Nope.

Walrus puppet? Nope.

I could go no farther. I was in the corner of the room, right underneath the big, misshapen model of the solar system that hung from the ceiling. We were told that some kid last year had made it out of old pennies and plastic wrap, for something called Science Night. It was terrible but too heavy to move, so Mr. Copeland left it up.

"Found you," said Beefer.

I turned. "Oh, hi, Beefer," I said, trying to sound casual.

"Now you must choose your destiny, Sam," he said. "Do you want Nerdsmasher?" He held out his left fist. "Or Dweebcrusher?" He held out his right fist.

"What are the pros and cons?" I said, playing for time.

"Quit stalling, Sam."

"Okay, fine. Did you say one was called Nerdsmoosher?"

"Nerd*smasher*! Nerdsmoosher would be a ridiculous name for a fist."

"Right, sorry . . ."

From the corner of my eye I saw movement up above me. Something was running along the strings of the solar system model.

"In that case," I said. "I'm thinking maybe Dweebcruncher?"

"It's Dweeb*crusher*!" yelled Beefer. "It's like you're not taking this situation seriously! That makes me so—"

Both of us heard a growl.

CHAPTER 3

"**H**EY LOOK, IT'S the dumb, barking gerbil," said Beefer. He stared up at Hamstersaurus Rex, who was clinging to the string that held the solar system, directly above Beefer's head.

"Hamstersaurus Rex," I said.

Beefer turned to glare at me. "Martha Junior," he said.

"Right, sorry. Martha Junior."

Above him, Hamstersaurus Rex began to chew on the string.

"Now, where were we?" said Beefer.

"Um, I think you had decided that violence is

never the answer and you were about to let me go with a stern warning."

Beefer scratched his head, confused. "Are you sure? Because that doesn't really sound like something I'd—"

There was a snap. Then a crash. And Beefer Vanderkoff was lying flat on the ground under a pile of plastic-wrap-and-penny planets. I blinked. Hamstersaurus Rex had gnawed clean through the string. He'd saved me!

"Mom . . . are we at Grandma's yet?" moaned Beefer. If he could moan, he wasn't dead. Which was good. Sort of. I guess.

"Thanks!" I said to Hamstersaurus Rex, still dangling from the string on the ceiling. I held my hands out to catch him. "Now, why don't you come on down from there?"

And that's what he did. Except instead of jumping into my outstretched hands, he dropped right onto the top of my head. Which—even though I'm pretty pro-hamster—felt *super weird* and I, uh, *may* have screamed. A lot. And this *may* have scared Hamstersaurus Rex. Which is probably why he scurried down my back and squeezed underneath the door of the classroom.

"Sorry! I have a very sensitive scalp!" I cried. "Please don't go!"

But he didn't wait. Out in the hall once again, I caught a flash of his furry orange butt disappearing around a corner. I ran as fast as I could, but Hamstersaurus Rex was faster. He darted down the stairs, and I followed. By the time I made it to the end of the hallway, he was nowhere to be seen.

I stood at the door of the school gymnasium: this *had* to be where Hamstersaurus Rex had gone. My watch said ten till four. My mom would be by to pick me up any minute. Still, I couldn't just let Hamstersaurus Rex disappear again.

Inside the gym it was dark and quiet. I squinted. Was that a flash of movement racing toward Coach Weekes's office? I ran toward the door and threw it open.

The lights were on. Coach Weekes, our mustachioed gym teacher, stood facing a full-length mirror. He held a protein shake in one hand and an old-fashioned trophy in the other. He didn't see me.

"And now, representing the town of Maple Bluffs at the Regional Personal Fitness Championship," said Coach Weekes in a strange announcer voice, "Leslie Weekes, a.k.a. the Velvet Shark."

Coach Weekes took a swig of the protein shake and then flexed all the muscles he had. He didn't have many.

Again, in the announcer voice: "Wow, will you

look at that physique, folks? I wouldn't be surprised if Weekes is awarded the Special Jury Prize for 'Best Calf Muscles.' Looks like he's got two hams stuffed into his socks, doesn't it? You know, the winner of this competition will go on to nationals and will probably become famous and rich and no one will ever laugh at his mustache ever again! Weekes is the *strong* favorite—pun intended—because, as we all know, he's already a winner."

Weekes held up his old trophy and smiled into the mirror, then flexed some more. I slowly took a step backward. One of the floorboards creaked. Coach Weekes whipped around. He looked mortified.

"Gibbs!" he said. "What are you doing here? My office is my personal— School let out twenty minutes— Er, why are you— Gibbs!"

"Sorry," I said. "I, uh, thought this was the bathroom?"

"Well, it's not! And next time you should knock, because I'm doing important coach stuff in here! Good manners are part of fitness, too, you know!"

"Right. Sorry," I said again. I turned to go. But as I did, something caught my eye.

In a hole at the base of the wall, beside Coach Weekes's mirror, I saw a tiny pair of black eyes looking back at me.

"What are you gawking at, Gibbs?" asked Coach Weekes.

"Your trophy," I lied, pointing to the one in his hand.

Coach Weekes gazed at it lovingly. The trophy had a sculpture on top: an angry-looking child with the build of a superhero. Weekes smiled. "Little Mister Muscles. Won it when I was your age, for general physical excellence. Knuckle-ups! The Sixty-Foot Sandbag Drag! Now *that* was a real competition!"

"Wow, knuckle-ups? That sounds, uh, really awesome," I lied, stalling as I inched toward the hole in the wall. "I wish we had, you know, something like that today."

Coach Weekes stroked his mustache. "You know, Gibbs, that's not a half-bad idea."

"You really think so, Coach?" I said. I was barely a foot from the hole now. I crouched down and reached out my hand—

"Sam?"

I turned. It was my mom.

"I've been looking everywhere for you," she said, frowning. "Why weren't you in the library?"

"Sorry," I said. "I, uh, thought this was the bathroom."

Coach Weekes shot my mom a concerned look. She sighed.

"Okay, well, it's time to ah . . ." My mom froze. "It's time to, ah . . . ah, ACHOOOOO!" And she sneezed, which is the loudest sound my mom ever makes. I can't say for sure, but it might be the loudest sound known to science. Coach Weekes and I both jumped a foot into the air.

"Sorry," said my mom, wiping her nose. "I must be allergic to something."

"Muscles?" said Coach Weekes hopefully.

"I don't think so," she said.

As far as I know, my mom is allergic to one thing: furry animals. It's the reason we have a hairless cat instead of, oh, I don't know, a hamster.

Speaking of no hamsters: when I turned to look at the hole again, Hamstersaurus Rex wasn't there.

CHAPTER 4

THE NEXT MORNING, before school, Beefer caught me alone in the hallway. He's usually twenty minutes late to homeroom. Early Beefer wasn't a good sign. I could see a lump the size of a golf ball on the top of his head. The guy was angry. Granted, Beefer Vanderkoff is always angry. But today, he was extra, super mega-angry. At me.

"Fine morning we're having, isn't it, Sam?" he said, glancing around for adults. Of course, whenever you needed them, there weren't any.

"Sam? Oh no. You have made a large confusion," I said, trying my best to do an accent. "I am his identical cousin, Jarmo. From Finland!"

"That's not going to work a second time," said Beefer.

He grabbed me by the arm and yanked me, once more, into the second-floor boys' bathroom. Someone had righted the trash can Beefer punched, but it still bore the dent from his clear belt karate demonstration. I worried that my face would soon have a similar dent.

"First off," said Beefer, holding me by the collar, "you tell anybody what happened, that I got KO'd by a gerbil, you're dead."

"I didn't see any gerbil," I said. Technically true.

"Anybody asks, I was minding my own business, vandalizing the school, when those dumb planets randomly fell on my head. Got it?"

"Sure. Just an innocent act of vandalism," I said. "Could've happened to anyone."

"Second," said Beefer, "when I find Martha Junior, he's going to pay."

"Hey, come on, Beefer," I said. "You don't need to worry about Hamstersaurus Rex. He's just an animal. He didn't—"

"I've seen the little posters you drew. I know

you *love* that rodent. But I live by a very simple code, Sam. That code is: nobody drops a home-made solar system on Beefer Vanderkoff and gets away with it. *Nobody*."

"I admire how specific your code is," I said. "But there's really no need to—"

"Enough gum-flapping," he said, gripping my collar tighter. "I want to tell you about your special surprise."

"A Caribbean vacation?"

"Nope. But it does involve water," said Beefer with a yellow smile. He kicked open the door to one of the bathroom stalls. "You're familiar with the regular old swirlie, of course."

I sighed. "Sure. The thing where you flush the toilet and stick my head in it." A swirlie is pretty awful, but probably not as bad as getting my face punched in. When you're me, unfortunately, you have to rank these things.

"See, that's just the problem," said Beefer, putting his arm around me. "You're *used* to swirlies. And that means we need something new. Last night—as I was lying in bed and rubbing this giant, painful bump on my head—I started thinking: How can I take the swirlie to the next level? How can I leave my own mark on a classic?"

"You're considering your bullying legacy," I said. "Great."

"That's when I came up with what I call the 'Kiefer Beefer Vanderkoff Ultra-Swirlie,' or the 'KiBeVaUl-Swi' for short."

"KiBeVaUl-Swi," I said. "Really rolls off the tongue."

"The KiBeVaUl-Swi is just like a regular swirlie," said Beefer, "except for one important innovation."

Beefer reached into his pocket and pulled out a twenty-four-ounce bag of Uncle Puckett's Powdered Pancake Mix (A SmilesCorp Product™). He tore the bag open, flushed the toilet, then dumped the powder in. It formed a swirling beige sludge in the bowl.

I frowned. "Is it too late for you to just punch me?"

"We'll get to that," said Beefer. "But first, your KiBeVaUl-Swi!"

And with that, he flipped me upside down.

"Please, Beefer, I have a very sensitive scalp!"

Beefer was unmoved. He dunked my head into the swirling goop. When he pulled me out, I was covered down to my shoulders in sticky, toilet-made pancake batter.

"Well?" said Beefer. He was waiting for his first customer review.

"It's awful," I said, wiping the stuff out of my eyes.

"Fantastic," said Beefer. And with that, he slugged me in the gut, knocking the wind out of me.

"It's only a matter of time before I find Martha Junior," he said as he turned to leave. "I'm going to take him home and feed him to my pet boa constrictor. He's a dead gerbil walking."

I thought of seven or eight snappy comebacks but neglected to share them. I sure didn't want another KiBeVaUl-Swi.

And so I spent the next fifteen minutes trying to clean off pancake batter in the sink. It doesn't come out as easily as you think. In fact, while I was washing my face, my swirlied hair hardened into a weird, crusty spike. No matter how much I tried to flatten it, the shape kept reforming. The bell rang, and I had to go to class looking like the world's saddest unicorn.

World's Saddest unicorn   Me

"Very avant-garde hairstyle, Sam," said Mr. Copeland.

"Thanks," I said, taking my seat.

"Not a compliment," said Mr. Copeland. He waited a moment until everyone was settled. "All right, kids, some of you have noticed that our classroom's model of the solar system is missing. That's because of an incident that happened after school." He squinted at Beefer, who pretended not to pay attention by leafing through the October issue of *Pustule*, the horror-movie special-effects magazine.

"Just to restate the obvious, none of you should be in this classroom unattended," said Mr. Copeland as he confiscated Beefer's magazine. "Got it?"

"Yes, Mr. Copeland," we all said in unison.

Tina Gomez raised her hand.

"What is it, Tina?" said Mr. Copeland.

"I don't know, Mr. Copeland. First we lose our class hamster, now our solar system model," she said, shaking her head dramatically. "What tragedy is *next*?"

"Tina, we had a 'class hamster' for less than ten minutes," said Mr. Copeland.

"We should really get some snails to replace him," said Wilbur Weber.

"More snails is your solution to every problem, Wilbur."

"Mr. Copeland, I have a theory," said Martha Cherie, smiling in a way that she must have thought was sweetly.

"Great. Here we go," said Mr. Copeland with a sigh.

"It may sound fanciful, but perhaps the two events are connected in some way," she said. "I mean, Hamstersaurus Rex's mysterious disappearance and the subsequent destruction of the solar system model, that is."

Beefer was now glaring at me with raw hatred in his eyes. I could see the lump on his head throbbing. I shrugged frantically to indicate that I hadn't told anyone he'd been KO'd by a gerbil.

"Sorry. No mystery here, Martha," said Mr. Copeland. "Kiefer was messing with the solar system when it fell on his head. He enjoys spending time in this classroom so much, Principal Truitt has given him after-school detention every Monday for the foreseeable future."

Beefer stretched and yawned to indicate boredom. Mr. Copeland gritted his teeth.

So Beefer and I were the only ones who knew the real truth. Despite his warnings, I had to tell somebody. I still had a hamster to find, and I figured two heads were better than one. So at lunch, I quietly recounted the solar system incident to the only person I could trust: Dylan D'Amato.

"Wow. Beefer Vanderkoff defeated by Hamstersaurus Rex," said Dylan after listening to the whole story. "Sam, does it bother you that you're not as tough as a hamster?"

"A little," I said.

Dylan and I had been best friends ever since the first week of preschool—when I got an empty sand pail stuck on my head and she was the only kid strong enough to yank it off. We were plenty different. She made fun of me a lot, but when anybody else did she got furious. I always nodded politely when she went on and on about disc golf.

I never laughed when she tried to draw stuff (even though every one of her pictures invariably ended up looking like a sweet potato with googly eyes).

Man

Cloud

Cat

Sun

Rabbit

"You should just stand up to Beefer," said Dylan.

"Uh-huh," I said. "And you'll cover the cost of my facial reconstruction surgery?"

"Nah, it's not like that," said Dylan. "Remember in second grade when you were scared to take baths because you thought a lobster was going to come up the drain?"

I sighed. "Yes, I remember."

"That's what Beefer is."

"An imaginary drain lobster?"

"I mean, if you're not afraid of him then he

doesn't have any power over you."

"What? Yes, he does. The power to punch me and stick me in pancake toilets and probably some other worse stuff that I haven't even thought of yet!"

"I know, but if you're not *afraid* of getting punched—"

"But I *am* afraid of it," I said. "It hurts. A lot."

"Okay, fine. Look, if you want me to, I can kick his butt on your behalf. I've got some free time this afternoon." She demonstrated a little shadowboxing.

"You can't fight my battles for me, Dylan. I'm going to handle this one the good old-fashioned Sam Gibbs way: with plenty of cowardice and a dash of hiding," I said. "Anyway, forget about Beefer. I'm just glad Hamstersaurus Rex is okay."

"You sure love that weird hamster, huh?"

"As much as you love disc golf."

"Wow," said Dylan, nodding with newfound respect. "That's a lot."

I told her about seeing Hamstersaurus Rex flee into the gymnasium.

"Living in Coach Weekes's office, huh? I sure hope the little dude likes the smell of weight gainers and feet," said Dylan. "We should tell Mr. Copeland—"

"What? No way!" I said. "Beefer's out for revenge. If Hamstersaurus Rex goes back into the cage in our classroom, he'll be a sitting duck. Beefer will get him for sure! In fact, now I have to find Hamstersaurus Rex before Beefer does."

"Maybe during gym class, you can figure out a way to sneak into Weekes's office and rescue him," she suggested.

"Good thinking," I said. "Just promise me you won't tell anybody about any of this, okay?"

Dylan laughed. "Sam, when have I *ever* spilled a secret?"

I cocked my head. "What about the time you let it slip that my mom calls me Bunnybutt?"

"Sorry about that," she said. "I mean, it's not the *worst* nickname."

I frowned. "Just keep this quiet, all right."

"Keep what quiet?" asked Martha Cherie. She'd appeared out of nowhere, like some sort of honor-student ghost.

"Nothing!" I said. "I mean, uh, I was just telling Dylan to keep it quiet, when she plays her, uh, trombone. We play together. In a band. It's Dylan on trombone and me on, uh . . ."

"Washboard," said Dylan.

"Right," I said. "A classic trombone and washboard duo. If she plays too loud, it drowns me out." I smiled and pantomimed a wicked air washboard solo.

"Wow, Sam," said Martha, "I knew you were really creative, ever since you drew that beautiful portrait of me last year."

"You mean the *caricature* where Sam made your nose look like an overripe beet?" said Dylan in disbelief.

"Uh-huh. I love beets," said Martha. "So what's

the name of your band?"

"The Dylan D'Amato Experience," said Dylan, crossing her arms and squinting at her. "Very hip. You probably wouldn't get it."

"Is that why you have a flamboyant new rock 'n' roll hairstyle?" said Martha. She was looking at my crusty pancake hair-horn.

"Uh-huh," I said, fluffing it up a little. "Pretty edgy, huh?"

"You look like a narwhal," said Martha. "It's my favorite northern-latitudes sea mammal."

I gave her a thumbs-up. Dylan rolled her eyes four, maybe five, times.

Narwhal   Me

"Anyway, I wanted to share some information with you, Sam, since you seem to be concerned about the fate of our beloved class pet." Martha held up one of my Hamstersaurus Rex posters. "Perhaps I shouldn't even be telling you this, as it's part of an ongoing Hamster Monitor investigation—"

"Hamster Monitor isn't a real thing," said Dylan. "You know that, right?"

Martha held up her ID lanyard as proof. "Like I said earlier, I think the solar system falling and Hamstersaurus Rex disappearing are related."

"What?" I said with a forced, high-pitched laugh. "No way." If Martha connected the dots, Beefer would assume I told her. Then he would pound me.

"I was able to recover the piece of string from

_," said Martha. She held it up. "I ex-
_ the frayed end under a microscope in
_ science lab. It appears to have been _gnawed_.
What if Hamstersaurus Rex did that?"

"Come on!" I said, panicking. "You're joking.
Ha-ha. You're so funny, Martha. Did anyone ever
tell you that?"

She smiled. "No. When people compliment
me, it's usually on my above-average intelligence,
my punctuality, or my commitment to flossing."

"Oh, please," muttered Dylan.

"Well, personally, I think Hamstersaurus Rex
is gone for good," I said. "Probably just as well. I
like to think of him out there in the wilderness
somewhere. Maybe he joined a pack of wild hamsters. Running free across the tundra—"

"No," said Martha. "I have reason to believe
that Hamstersaurus Rex is still living somewhere
within the school. In fact, I believe I know his approximate location."

"Where?" I said.

"I'm not at liberty to disclose that information," said Martha.

"Come on. You have no idea where he is," said Dylan.

"Do too," said Martha. "He's in the boiler room."

"Wrong," said Dylan.

What was Dylan doing? I tried to catch her eye but she ignored me.

"That's pretty unlikely," said Martha, "because I've never been wrong before."

Dylan snapped. "Oh, come on! The boiler room? *The boiler room!* That's all the way on the other side of the school from the gym!"

"So . . . you think Hamstersaurus Rex is in the gym?" said Martha. She already had her notebook out and she was scribbling something. I turned to stare at Dylan. She had both hands capped over her mouth.

"I mean, uh, who knows?" said Dylan quietly. "He could be in the . . . library."

"I have all I need for now," said Martha, smiling as she turned away. "Thanks, Dylan."

CHAPTER 5

RAIN PELTED THE gymnasium windows.

"Look, Sam, I'm really sorry," said Dylan. "I definitely didn't mean to give up Hamstersaurus Rex's location."

"This is worse than Bunnybutt," I said, shaking my head.

"I know."

"This is even worse than that time in first grade"—I dropped my voice low—"when you told everyone I had *an accident*."

"What?" cried Dylan. "That wasn't me! I didn't tell *anyone* you pooped your pants!"

"Shh!" I said, wincing. "Look, it's all in the past now. Anyway, maybe Martha wasn't listening when you told her exactly where to find Hamster-saurus Rex."

The two of us were in phys ed class, taught by Coach Weekes. I hoped that I might find a moment to sneak away and look for Hamstersaurus Rex in his office. Preferably before anyone else got there first.

Despite her remorse, I could tell Dylan was excited for today. We were going to start a whole week of disc golf—the sport where you throw circular discs at various targets to score points. As I mentioned, disc golf was Dylan's absolute favorite thing in the world. She'd even brought her own discs from home. They were officially certified for tournament play.

"All right, everybody," said Coach Weekes, blowing his whistle. "Disc golf is out."

"What?" cried Dylan. "How come?"

"Because it's not a real sport, D'Amato."

"Is too," said Dylan. "Disc golf is played in over forty countries worldwide. By 2031, it will be more popular than devil sticks!" Dylan had a premium subscription to *Disc Golf Online*.

"Enough *facts*, D'Amato," said Weekes. "I'm

43

the one teaching physical education, so leave the *educating* to me. Anyway, what we're going to do instead is way better."

"Fight each other with real swords?" asked Jared Kopernik.

"Maybe next term, Kopernik," said Coach Weekes. "No, we're going to participate in a class-wide physical fitness competition called Little Mister Muscles." Coach Weekes held up his dusty trophy with the grimacing hulk-child on top.

I sighed. Like I said, I'm not the most athletic student at Horace Hotwater Middle School. Any contest of physical fitness was bound to be humiliating.

"Little *Mister* Mucles?" said Julie Bailey. "Coach, half of us are girls."

"Fair point, Bailey. So the new name is Little Mister *or* Miss Muscles. But that's the *only* change I'm making. Otherwise it's going to be the exact same competition it was in 1983, when I won it. Right before it was discontinued in 1984 for legal reasons."

"Why was it discontinued in 1984 for legal reasons?" I asked.

"Not sure. Some kid lost an ear or something. Don't worry about it, Gibbs. Anyway, I made a few calls this morning, and SmilesCorp—manufacturers of some of my favorite health and dietary supplements—is going to sponsor Little Mister or Miss Muscles. They ponied up for a new trophy. Winner's going to be awarded it on Science Night."

I knew SmilesCorp well. That's where my mom works as an accountant. They make everything from the aforementioned Funchos Flavor-Wedges to video games to orbital satellites. The company probably employs a third of the people who live in Maple Bluffs.

"Now," said Coach Weekes as he lovingly polished the trophy with the corner of his shirt. "Does anybody have any questions? Perhaps you'd like to know more about the various feats of prowess that earned yours truly the coveted title of Little Mister Muscles?"

Dylan raised her hand.

"Question, D'Amato," said Coach Weekes.

"Coach, did you know that there are some three thousand disc golf courses in the United States and over four thousand more worldwide?"

"Drop it! I'm talking *real* tests of fitness here: Knuckle-ups! Rod Bends! The Sixty-Foot Sandbag Drag! The classics."

"Well I've never heard of any of them," said Dylan. "So maybe those are the *real* made-up sports!"

Coach Weekes clutched the trophy close, and his mustache fluttered like he might burst into tears. "If you don't like it, D'Amato, I suggest you take it up with your pal Gibbs. Bringing back Little Mister or Miss Muscles was his idea in the first place!"

The whole class turned to stare at me. They didn't look happy.

"Okay, how about this, Coach," said Dylan, gritting her teeth. "If I win Little Mister or Miss

Muscles, then we play disc golf for a whole month. How's that sound?"

"Fine," said Coach Weekes. "If you win, we can play whatever crazy non-sport you want for the rest of the *year*! It can be tic-tac-toe for all I care! Now, everybody pair off and grab a medicine ball. You're going to need to build your glute strength for the Sandbag Drag. Little Mister or Miss Muscles is happening next week. Mark your calendars!"

"I can't believe Weekes," said Dylan as we tossed a thirty-pound medicine ball back and forth. "Disc golf is a real sport. One day I'm going to play in the majors. When there are majors."

"Sorry I accidentally suggested this weird competition to him," I said, catching the ball with a grunt. "I was just trying to distract him long enough to grab—"

A flash of movement over Dylan's shoulder caught my eye: a little orange shape scurried along the base of the gymnasium wall toward Coach Weekes's office. Sure enough, it was Hamstersaurus Rex!

I looked around to see if anybody else had

noticed him. Nobody had . . . nobody except Beefer Vanderkoff, that is.

Our eyes met. Beefer smiled. Then he reared back to lob his medicine ball right at the hamster. He was going to flatten the little guy!

I had to do something. As Beefer heaved the ball, I dove.

"Sam," cried Dylan, "what are you—"

I threw myself right in the medicine ball's path. *KA-THWAP!* My vision went white as the ball ricocheted off my head and flew high into the air. It hung there for a moment and then fell, landing right on Coach Weekes's Little Mister Muscles trophy and smashing it to bits.

I lay on the floor, dazed. After a moment, I sat up to see that Hamstersaurus Rex was gone. The whole gym was silent, except for a quiet sobbing noise. It was Coach Weekes.

"Who threw that?" he said,

eyes welling with tears as he looked down at what remained of his trophy. Outside, thunder crashed.

Nobody said a word, but Beefer and Jimmy Choi were the only pair without a medicine ball. Jimmy stared at his feet.

"Vanderkoff," snarled Coach Weekes.

"I wasn't trying to hit him. Dumb nerd just got in the way," said Beefer. "I was actually aiming for, uh, nothing. Whatever. Never mind. Everybody shut up."

"I don't care *what* you were *trying* to do, Vanderkoff!" said Coach Weekes. "Choi is standing right in front of you, yet you managed to throw your medicine ball twenty feet in the wrong direction and destroy my trophy!"

"Uh, he also hit Sam in the face," said Dylan.

"Not now, D'Amato!" said Coach Weekes, sniffling yet barely managing to contain his rage. "Do you have *anything* else to say for yourself, Vanderkoff?"

Beefer gave a surly shrug. "School sucks."

"You're going to Principal Truitt's office right now!" said Coach Weekes, and he marched Beefer right out of the gym, leaving the class unattended.

"Sam, you look worse than the time you accidentally ate that grasshopper," said Dylan as she helped me up. "Are you all right?"

"I think so," I said. "My pancake hair spike absorbed most of the force." Indeed, my hairstyle had finally been flattened.

"So, what do we do now?" asked Tina Gomez.

"Let's fight each other with real swords," suggested Jared Kopernik.

"How about disc golf until Coach gets back," said Dylan. "I'll teach you guys the basics." And so the class started an impromptu pickup game with the discs Dylan had brought from home. Not me, though. Now was my chance. While Coach Weekes was out, I could try to find Hamstersaurus Rex.

When I was sure nobody was watching, I quietly opened the door to his office. It was dark inside. But suddenly someone was shining a flashlight into my eyes.

"Stop right there," came a loud voice.

"Sorry, I thought this was the bathroom!" I said.

"Oh, hi, Sam," said Martha Cherie, lowering her flashlight. "I'm here on official Hamster Monitor business." She flashed her ID again. "I think Dylan was right. I think this might be where Hamstersaurus Rex is living." Martha held up a plastic bag she'd labeled "Evidence." Inside it was a half-eaten SmilesCorp Total NutriSlam protein bar. The wrapper had been chewed through.

"What?" I said. "Nah. Coach Weekes was, uh, probably just saving that half for later."

"Really?" She shined her flashlight down at the hole where I'd seen Hamstersaurus Rex before. "Because I found it stuffed inside the wall."

"Weekes is a weird guy."

Martha crouched beside the hole and shined her light in it. "I can only see a little ways in, but it's *full* of food wrappers."

"On second thought, you should keep looking. I bet he's in there," I said. Because at that moment—on the shelf above Martha's head—I saw a muffin-size rodent feasting on Coach Weekes's weird dietary supplements. It was Hamstersaurus Rex.

CHAPTER 6

MARTHA LEAPED TO her feet. "Nope, I don't think the fugitive is in the area."

"The fugitive?" I said.

"Hamstersaurus Rex, silly," she said. "As an officer of the law, I'm fully authorized to use all necessary measures to recapture the fugitive."

"Officer of the law?"

"Duh. Hamster Monitor," she said as she pointed to the ID lanyard again. "Now, I'm going to have to stake out this location and wait for him to come back. Maybe set up a perimeter."

Directly behind her head, the tiny "fugitive" continued to gobble Coach Weekes's odd supplements.

He was now gorging himself on a greenish Smiles-Corp bodybuilding powder. Something called Dinoblast Powerpacker.

"So, uh, hey, Martha," I said, trying to hold her attention so she wouldn't turn around. "I know you like narwhals and, uh, being a hamster super-cop, but what are some of your *other* interests?"

Martha cocked her head. "I have a collection of antique dolls. I find it extremely satisfying not to play with them."

"Wow. Neat!" I said.

"You know, Sam, if you're really interested in learning more about doll collecting—which isn't just a hobby but also an investment—we could visit the Antique Doll Museum."

By now, Hamstersaurus Rex had eaten most of the container of Powerpacker. He looked wobbly and sick. I shuddered to think what consuming half a pound of powdered bodybuilding supplement might do to a human, much less a hamster.

"A whole museum full of dusty old dolls," I said, trying to think of a way to distract Martha so I could grab Hamstersaurus Rex. "That sounds awesome! If anything, I worry that I'd want to spend too much time there."

"You can stay for up to nine hours before the security guard asks you to leave. They have an original Ginny Gossamer, famous for being history's most fragile doll. Definitely worth the price of admission to see a G.G. in person," said Martha. "We could even ride my tandem bicycle there together!"

Hamstersaurus Rex had keeled over. Why did he eat all that stuff? Was he some sort of fitness buff? He was starting to twitch now. He looked like he might be dying. I had to help him fast.

"Okay, yes, let's go to that," I said, racking my brain for a way to rescue him.

"You're not just going to back out at the last minute?" said Martha, cocking her head.

"Nope, I promise. Seriously, tandem bicycles are my favorite because they're, uh, not weird."

"I'll pencil you in for the thirtieth then."

"Absolutely. Wait, is *that* Hamstersaurus Rex?"

I pointed to the floor behind Coach Weekes's desk.

"Freeze!" bellowed Martha as she whirled and shined her flashlight in that direction. Behind her back, I scooped up Hamstersaurus Rex and tucked him into my pocket.

"False alarm. Just an old gym sock," said Martha, holding one up. "I'll bag it as evidence."

"Great," I said. "Got to go!"

I dashed out of the office, ran across the gym—where Dylan was humiliating the rest of the class at disc golf—and ducked into the janitor's closet. There, I pulled Hamstersaurus Rex out of my pocket. Lightning flashed outside.

The little guy looked gravely ill. He was breathing fast. His eyes were fluttering, and

green foam was bubbling up
at the corners of his mouth. I
didn't know what to do. If only
they taught *use-*
ful subjects in
school—like
hamster first
aid—instead
of math or
whatever!

"Come on," I said. "Don't die on me!"

His breathing slowed and then seemed to stop altogether. His body felt rigid. How do you check a hamster's pulse? I listened for a heartbeat. Nothing.

"Don't die," I whispered. "Don't die. Don't die."

But he was still. I felt him growing cold in my hands now. I didn't know what else to do, so I clutched him close to my chest, under my shirt for warmth. The seconds crawled by. I couldn't believe I'd found Hamstersaurus Rex, only to watch him eat poison and die before my eyes. It wasn't fair!

"If you pull through this, I promise I'll look

out for you," I said. "I'll take care of you and I'll feed you whatever you want, as long as it's not dietary supplements. And I'll never let anybody hurt you—"

A thunderclap rattled the window. Suddenly, Hamstersaurus Rex shuddered inside my shirt. He was alive! The little guy was alive!

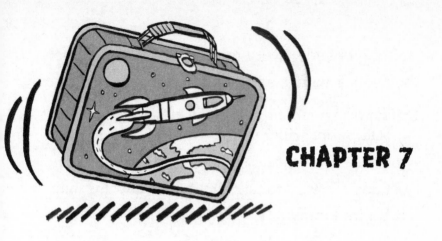

CHAPTER 7

DYLAN SQUINTED AT me from across the backseat of the car. On some days, my mom works late and Dylan's dad gives me a ride home. I tried to act normal, but Dylan knew something was up.

"Sam, I'm really sorry for being a blabbermouth before," she said.

"No problem," I said. "I already forgot about it." I smiled and gripped my lunch box tightly.

"And you're *sure* there's nothing, like, weird going on."

"Nope. Nothing. Hey, beautiful weather we're having!" I pointed out the window. It was still raining outside. Every once in a while my lunch box shook wildly, and I had to lean hard on it to keep it still.

"Oh, stop grilling him, Dylan," said her dad from the front seat. "Whatever it is, maybe he just doesn't want to talk about. Like how his mom calls him Bunnybutt."

"Dude. You told your dad about that?" I whispered.

"Yeah, sorry," said Dylan.

The truth was I *couldn't* tell Dylan that Hamstersaurus Rex was currently rattling around inside my lunch box. I felt terrible about it, but I was worried Dylan would spill the beans again. I couldn't risk it.

And I couldn't leave Hammie Rex at school, either. The little guy was alive but far from well. Plus Martha was taking her Hamster Monitor duties *way* too seriously. If she found the "fugitive" and locked him up in the cage in our classroom, Beefer would be able to get his revenge.

The way I saw it, I only had one option.

"Home sweet home, Sam," said Mr. D'Amato as

he pulled over to the curb.

"Thanks for the ride, Mr. D! See you later, Dylan!" I hopped out of the car.

"Okay," said Dylan. "Let me know if you want any help on your Science Night project."

"Science what now?" I said.

"Science Night," said Dylan. "The bimonthly science fair sponsored by SmilesCorp. Coming up in two weeks. Half your science grade depends on it. You *have* started on your project, right?"

"Um . . . yes?" I said unconvincingly. "I'll tell you all about it tomorrow. It's going to revolution-ize the field of . . . science!"

"Cool," said Dylan, looking concerned.

"Bye!" I said.

Once inside, I ran upstairs—past Raisin, my mom's twenty-three-year-old hairless cat who sleeps approximately twenty-four hours a day—and into my bedroom. I closed the door behind me, took a deep breath, and opened the lunchbox.

I gasped. Hamstersaurus Rex looked . . . *different*. His stumpy little arms were even stumpier than before. His lips were curled back to reveal teeth—no

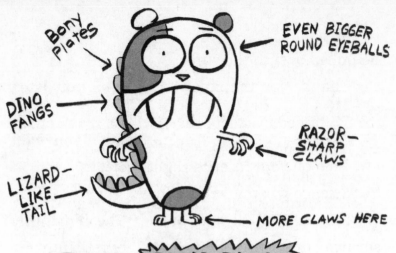

Bony Plates

EVEN BIGGER ROUND EYEBALLS

DINO FANGS

RAZOR-SHARP CLAWS

LIZARD-LIKE TAIL

MORE CLAWS HERE

POST DINO-BLAST HAMSTERSAURUS REX

longer square, but sharp little fangs. Most disturbing of all, he'd grown a little lizard-y tail that swayed from side to side behind him.

Hamstersaurus Rex had just been a silly name before, but now he really *did* look like he was part dinosaur. Had consuming the bizarre mixture of Dinoblast Powerpacker and other vitamins *mutated* him somehow? What was SmilesCorp putting in that stuff? The supplements didn't seem to be having the same effect on Coach Weekes, but then again, he *was* pretty weird in other ways.

Hamstersaurus Rex blinked at me.

"Uh," I said. "Are you . . . okay?"

In answer, he let out a thunderous Jurassic roar. I jumped five feet backward and may or may not have temporarily lost bladder control.

"Heh, heh, heh," I said, my voice trembling. "Nice Hamstersaurus. Good Hamstersaurus." It suddenly occurred to me that after his change, he might not be so friendly anymore.

Hamstersaurus hopped out of the lunch box and stomped toward me—he seemed to prefer walking on his back legs now. He gave a snarl.

I went limp and fell to the ground as if I were dead. I'd read somewhere that you were supposed to do this in case of a bear attack. I figured a mutant hamster-dinosaur hybrid attack was kind of like a bear attack because they both have, uh, feet?

I opened one eye and saw Hamstersaurus Rex spread his jaws wide. He chomped down on my finger! I squealed, but it didn't hurt. Much. The little guy was definitely gnawing on me, but in a friendly way.

"You only *sort of* want to eat me, huh?" I said.

He whined and wagged his tail and chewed a

little harder on my knuckle. Now it did hurt.

"Ow," I said, yanking my hand away. "Guess you must be hungry. Let me find you something to eat. Stay there." I closed the door behind me and went downstairs to the kitchen. I took a head of lettuce from the vegetable crisper and returned to my room.

"Bon appétit," I said, holding out a leaf toward Hamstersaurus Rex. "Leafy greens. Full of fiber. Hamster-licious but also hamster-tritious. Better than human fingers."

Hamstersaurus Rex nibbled a little. Then, in three big bites, he ate the whole leaf.

"Wow, you're starving. Mutating into a dinosaur probably burns a lot of calories." I held out another leaf. But Hammie Rex wasn't there. I turned around to see the little guy standing behind me on the bed. He'd already wolfed down the rest of the lettuce head.

"Dude," I said. "You're a straight-up salad slayer."

He looked up at me and growled plaintively. This time, the sound wasn't coming from his mouth. It was coming from his little belly.

"What? You're *still* hungry?" I said. "You just ate twice your weight in romaine."

He hopped off the bed and stomped toward the bedroom door and started scratching at it.

"No. Sorry, you have to stay in here," I said. "I can't have you shedding all over the house. My mom is *extremely* allergic to anything with fur. That's why our cat looks like a grandpa. And speaking of Raisin, hamsters and cats are natural enemies. For your own safety, I need to keep you two separated. Sit tight and I'll see if we have any more hamster snacks."

I ran downstairs and came back with a bag of green apples. One by one, Hamstersaurus Rex gobbled them down, core and all. He was still hungry.

"Look, we don't have any more food," I said when he was done. "Why don't you play with this yo-yo instead?"

I held out a yo-yo. Hamstersaurus Rex looked at it. He looked at me. Then he kicked the yo-yo. It hit the wall and broke into two pieces.

"Guess you're more of a Slinky guy," I said.

Hamstersaurus Rex sniffed the air and looked longingly at the door. He wanted out.

"Nope. I'm not going to resuscitate you just so you can get eaten by my geriatric family cat," I said.

Hamstersaurus Rex didn't listen. He backed up, pawed the ground a couple of times like a bull, and charged the door.

"Wait, stop, you'll hurt your—"

KA-BLAM! The little guy smashed his head into my bedroom door, hard, blasting it wide open. He didn't just have a dinosaur tail and dinosaur fangs, he had dinosaur strength, too!

"Dude, I think you broke the door!" I said, gaping at a

hand-sized splinter that had been knocked out of the frame.

But Hamstersaurus Rex had frozen in his tracks. In the hallway, I saw a pair of gleaming green eyes. It was Raisin! Her eyes were green? Weird. I'd never actually seen them open. My mom and I mostly know that Raisin is still alive because she sleeps in different locations around the house.

"Okay," I said, "everyone remain calm."

Raisin hissed.

"I think we can find a diplomatic solution to the current—"

Raisin pounced.

Hamstersaurus Rex reared back and un-leashed another earsplitting roar. Somehow, Raisin changed direction in midair. With a stran-gled yowl, she tore off down the hallway like a terrified flesh-colored lightning bolt. I heard

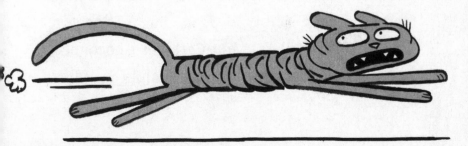

something break on the other side of the house.

"Stay right there until I get back!" I said to Hamstersaurus Rex. He hopped up and down and wagged his dino tail, like he thought it was a game.

I found Raisin wedged inside the filing cabinet in my mom's office. There were files all over the floor. She'd somehow managed to break the stapler, too.

"Sorry, girl," I said, trying to soothe and dislodge her at the same time. After a few minutes of tugging, I was finally able to get her unstuck. (Raisin gets kind of gummy on warmer days.) The old cat seemed to be medically unhurt but psychologically scarred. She immediately went to sleep.

I ran back to my bedroom, but there was no sign of Hamstersaurus Rex.

I found him downstairs in the kitchen. He'd knocked open the cupboard to get at my mom's forbidden strategic reserve of "hidden" junk food: Funchos Flavor-Wedges, Sugar Noshers, Spicy Cheez Wallets, Mint-Caramel Choconobs, and many more nutritionally empty goodies.

Hamstersaurus had torn into the packages, like some brutal nature show predator, and was feasting upon the processed innards of his prey.

"Dude!" I said. "How am I going to deal with this mess before my mom gets—"

I heard the sound of her car in the driveway. I sighed. If she checked the mail, I had about a minute and a half. In a flash, I cleaned up everything as best as I could and skidded to a halt in the foyer just as my mom's key scraped in the lock.

My mom opened the door holding some envelopes. "Hi, Bunnybutt, I'm home!"

"Hffffff," I wheezed. Sweat dripped from my forehead onto the floor.

"Wow, you're just . . . standing here in the dark panting, huh?" said my mom.

I nodded.

"That's not creepy at all," she said as she flicked on the light and headed toward the kitchen.

I still hadn't caught my breath. My mind raced. Had I remembered everything? Sugar Noshers packaging? Check. Shredded Cheez Wallet bags? Check. Choconob wrappers? Check. Yep, that was all of it. Except, wait, wasn't there something else?

Hamstersaurus Rex! Not check! Not check at all! The little guy was still at large. I made it to the kitchen just as my mom turned on the light.

But Hamstersaurus Rex was nowhere to be seen. I'd already started trying to talk my way out of the situation before I realized there wasn't one. "See, Mom, the thing is . . . ," I said, trailing off.

"Yes?" she said, looking skeptical.

"The thing is, um, I really like your scarf. Would you call that color 'maupe'?"

"That's not a color, Sam. But thank you," she said, cocking her head and squinting. "You know, something looks different in here." She sniffed the air and ran her finger along the counter.

I shrugged. Then shrugged again.

"Sam, be honest," she said. "Did you clean up the house?"

"Guilty as charged," I said, smiling a little too hard.

She smiled back at me. "Well, aren't you a good little ah, ah, ah, ACHOOOOO!" My mom sneezed. Again, this is debatably the loudest sound known to science. She wiped her nose, which was now bright red and running. "Oh, Sam, tell me you didn't bring some kind of furry animal into the—ACHOOOOOO!" She sneezed again.

"No way, Mom! Of course not. I know how allergic you are," I said, feeling particularly guilty as I handed her a tissue. "There might be a little dust in the air. I dusted."

"You did? Well aren't you . . . ACHOOOOO!"

When I made it back to my room, Hamstersaurus Rex was sitting on the floor. He'd strewn the contents of my backpack all over my room.

"Hey, come on, there's no food in there!" I said, closing the door behind me.

But he wasn't looking for food. He was standing on my open sketchbook, staring at a picture that I'd drawn—a picture of him.

"Yep," I said. "That's you."

He squinted at the picture, then back at me. He waggled his dino tail. He looked confused.

"Well, you're a little different now," I said. I grabbed a pencil and added a tail and fangs and used the eraser to redraw his arms stumpier. "There."

He looked at the new picture and burped. I took it to mean he was satisfied. Somewhere in the house, my mom sneezed.

"Look," I said, plopping down on the floor beside him. "I'm not sure you can stay here after all."

Hamstersaurus Rex whined and stared up at me, looking cute and innocent (well, as cute and innocent as a fanged hamster *can* look). My mom sneezed again. A framed poster of a spaceship fell off the wall.

"I wish you could live with me, but I don't think it's going to work. I guess I'm taking you back to school tomorrow. But you have to rein it in, though. Keep it low profile. Otherwise you're going to be in real danger. No more rampaging, okay?"

I drew a quick sketch of Hamstersaurus Rex rampaging and then a big X over it.

"See? No rampaging. Stay calm, like this."

Beside the first picture, I drew another of Hamstersaurus Rex calmly meditating and a big thumbs-up and a bunch of stars next to it. Hamstersaurus Rex looked at the two pictures for a minute. He blinked. Then he burped again.

I hoped we had an understanding.

CHAPTER 8

"Y **O, SAM!" SAID DYLAN** as she took her seat beside me in class.

"Shh!" I said. Hamstersaurus Rex was sound asleep in the pocket of my extra-baggy shirt, and I didn't want him to wake up.

"What? Why?" said Dylan.

"Um. I've—I've just got a headache. That's all." I rubbed my temples.

"Hmm. You *did* take a medicine ball to the skull. Maybe you have permanent brain damage," said Dylan cheerfully. "Quick, how many pasta salads am I holding up?"

Her hands were empty.

"Zero?"

"Correct! Great, no brain damage. Your head-ache is probably just from stress. You should play some disc golf. Studies show it can reduce stress by up to forty-seven percent."

"Studies, plural?"

"One study," she admitted. "Paid for by the American Disc Golf Council."

"Morning, kids," said Mr. Copeland as he entered the classroom.

The whole class greeted him loudly. I winced, but Hamstersaurus Rex kept on sleeping. He seemed to have recovered from all the mutating he did the day before, but I still wanted to keep an eye on the little guy. Today, I planned to keep him hidden in my pocket.

"My, you're looking very well today, Mr. Copeland," said Martha Cherie.

"Really? Because my car got towed and I had to walk seven miles to get here." He sighed and dropped his bag on the floor. "Kids, if I teach you nothing else in sixth grade, remember this: when you have outstanding parking tickets, you need to pay them in a timely manner."

A few kids wrote this down.

"All right," said Mr. Copeland, plopping down at his desk. "The Pilgrims. Where were we with those Pilgrims?"

And so we continued to learn about Plimouth Plantation and the Massachusetts Bay Colony. Hamstersaurus Rex slept all the way through the founding of Rhode Island. It wasn't until around eleven thirty that I felt him stir.

"Morning, sunshine," I whispered, scratching the top of his head with my finger. He blinked and yawned. Then he sniffed the air.

I heard a crinkling sound from the next desk over. Omar Powell was carefully unwrapping something under his desk. A flash of shiny green wrapper told me it was a Mint-Caramel Choconob. Omar saw me staring at him and shrugged. I shook my head. He frowned and kept unwrapping the candy.

Suddenly, my desk jumped a foot toward his. Omar and I stared at each other. It was Hamstersaurus Rex, pulling me from inside my own pocket! The little guy smelled SmilesCorp junk food. He was crazy for the stuff.

"Sorry," I whispered, scooting my seat back.

Omar was staring at me like I was insane now. "First you draw a picture of me where I look like a scared owl," he

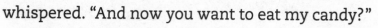

whispered. "And now you want to eat my candy?"

"I don't want to eat your candy!" I whispered. "And the drawing was nothing personal, I was just trying to learn how to do caricatures—"

"Sam!" said Mr. Copeland. "I'm assuming that you're so thrilled to learn more about how the Narraganset were subordinate to the Wampanoag Confederacy that you just can't contain yourself."

"Wampanoag Confederacy," I said, tapping my head. "Got it."

Mr. Copeland frowned and went back to

lecturing. Omar continued to unwrap the Cho-conob. I shook my head again and made a praying-hands gesture. Again Omar nodded and contin-ued peeling the wrapper. Once more, my desk lurched toward his—this time, two feet!

Hammie Rex was murmuring and wriggling. "Calm down!" I hissed into my pocket.

"*You* calm down!" whispered Omar.

"How about *both* of you calm down," said Mr. Copeland. "Now what seems to be the issue, gentlemen?"

I opened my mouth and a loud growl came out . . . of my pocket.

The whole class stared at me.

"Excuse me," I said, cover-ing my mouth. "I had, some, uh, bad tuna fish."

"For breakfast?" said Tina Gomez.

"Yep," I said, staring down at the ground. "For breakfast." I was trying to mentally will Hamstersaurus Rex to stay silent.

"Sam puts tuna on his cereal!" said Beefer.

"Now do you all see how weird this kid is?"

"Who asked you, Beefer?" said Dylan.

"Quiet, everybody!" said Mr. Copeland, exasperated.

"If I could address the class for just a moment," said Martha Cherie, standing. "I think everyone should know that tuna fish is an excellent source of protein and omega-3 fatty acids. In fact, all of you should probably be eating *more* tuna."

"Don't tell us how much tuna to eat," said Dylan, gritting her teeth. "I eat enough tuna. I eat loads and loads of tuna."

"Oh, then you might be eating too much, Dylan. You don't want to get mercury poisoning," said Martha. "Mr. Copeland, perhaps the class should have a designated Tuna Monitor to ensure that everybody eats the *right* amount of tuna and nobody gets mercury poisoning."

"Nope. That would be insane," said Mr. Copeland. "Now can we *please* get back to—"

"Um, speaking of mercury poisoning," said Jared Kopernik. "Can you get lead poisoning from eating a pencil?"

The whole class turned to stare at him now.

"No, Jared," said Mr. Copeland. "But . . . that doesn't mean it's good idea."

"Yeah, no. Of course not," said Jared with a high-pitched, nervous laugh. I couldn't help but notice that there was no pencil on his desk.

That's when the lunch bell rang. I sped out the door before Hamstersaurus Rex could growl again.

CHAPTER 9

"UGH! I CAN'T believe she wants to be the tuna police, too," said Dylan, glaring at the back of Martha Cherie's head in the cafeteria line. "She thinks she knows *everything*."

With all the mayhem and sneezing at home, I'd forgotten to pack a lunch like normal.

"Hey, did you ever get to look in Coach Weekes's office for Hamstersaurus Rex?" asked Dylan.

"He's not in there," I said with a shrug. It was true. Technically. That didn't make me feel much better for deceiving my best friend. "His office had a bunch of weird dietary supplements and a loose sock."

"Sounds about right," said Dylan. "Too bad. Let me know if you want help looking for him. I'd love to find him before Martha does. Beat her at her own game."

I wanted to tell her everything. "Actually, Hamstersaurus Rex is . . ."

"Is what?" said Dylan.

"Is probably long gone by now. I like to think he hitched a ride on a train bound for parts unknown. Maybe he's out there, riding the rails of this great land of ours, staring up at the—"

Hamstersaurus Rex growled. Dylan stared at me.

"Sorry," I said. "Breakfast tuna."

In the cafeteria line I picked up an extra hamburger for Hammie Rex. I put my tray down on the table beside Dylan's. Then I pretended I forgot the mustard, so I could sneak off. I ducked behind a stack of chairs and waited until I was sure nobody was watching.

"Okay, pal," I said, stuffing the hamburger into my pocket for him to gobble. "Here's lunch, but you've got to make it—"

Three bites and Hamstersaurus Rex was already done and whining for more.

"Last," I said.

I went back through the line again. "Can I have another hamburger, please?" I said to Judy, the lunch lady.

"You've got quite an appetite, son," said Judy, dropping one onto my tray.

"Actually, can you make it *three* extra hamburgers?" I said. "I'm trying to bulk up for Little Mister or Miss Muscles." I flexed.

"Looks like you need it," she said. And she served me two more hamburgers.

I sat down at Dylan's table.

"You know what," I said, "now I forgot ketchup!" I leaped up, carrying the stack of burgers.

"Sam, wait," called Dylan after me. "If you're feeling sick to your stomach, maybe eating *five* hamburgers isn't the greatest idea."

I pretended I didn't hear her and hid behind the chair stack again. I stuffed three more hamburgers into my pocket for Hamstersaurus Rex. He scarfed them, but still he wanted more! I went back through the line and asked Judy for another burger.

"Legally," said Judy, "I'm not sure I'm allowed to serve one kid six hamburgers."

"Please," I said. "I forgot to eat breakfast."

"I thought you ate tuna for breakfast," said Tina Gomez, who was getting a fruit cup.

"The tuna was a pre-breakfast snack," I said. "To tide me over until . . . lunch?"

"Son, that makes absolutely no sense," said Judy.

But she grudgingly served me one more burger. Hamstersaurus Rex was more than happy to eat it. His appetite seemed to defy the laws of physics. But at last, the little guy seemed satisfied. He growled and nuzzled my hand and poked his head out of my pocket to get a look around the cafeteria.

"Low profile," I said, gently pushing him back down with my finger.

I finished my own lunch just before the bell rang. Dylan looked at me funny the whole time.

The rest of the day passed pretty uneventfully. Hamstersaurus Rex was full and kept quiet. He didn't fling me around from inside my pocket anymore, either. Yay!

I realized that the key to preventing him from going berserk was keeping him fed. As long as he wasn't hungry he stayed calm, pleasant even. Simple enough.

After school, I made my way to the library to wait for my mom to pick me up. I gave it a minute, then I offered up some excuse to the librarian—my excuse count was off the charts these days—and I snuck off to my locker to deploy the second phase of my plan. The hallway was totally empty. Perfect.

I reached into my backpack and pulled out two bags of sand I'd brought from my mom's garden. I emptied the sand into the bottom of my locker. Then I pulled out more set dressing: dozens of toy dinosaurs and some plastic palm trees from an old fish tank I had. (One of several hairless pets that didn't quite work out. RIP Gill-iam Shakespeare.)

Last of all I taped a picture I'd drawn of an exploding volcano to the inside of my locker as a backdrop. In all the illustrations I'd seen in books, it seemed that dinosaurs *loved* hanging out around exploding volcanoes. Also in meteor showers.

When I was done, I had created a miniature prehistoric landscape inside my locker.

"All right, pal," I said to Hamstersaurus Rex, taking him out of my pocket and gently placing him into the locker. "This is where you'll be staying the night. I figured that since you're half dinosaur now, maybe this would make you feel at home."

Hamstersaurus Rex looked around. He looked at me. His lips pulled back in a weird little smile. I smiled back. He cuddled up next to a plastic parasaurolophus and gurgled.

"I'll take that as a yes," I said. "See you tomorrow, my friend." I stooped down and kissed him on top of the head (I may seem like a tough guy, but I'm actually pretty in touch with my emotions). I shut my locker door.

"Who were you just talking to?" said Beefer, stepping out from behind a water fountain a little ways down the hall.

"Nobody," I said, my heart racing. "Just, uh, my geometry book."

"You kiss your geometry book good night?"

"Yeah. I—I love geometry." I shrugged. "I may seem like a tough guy, but I'm actually pretty in touch with—"

"Shut it. Martha Junior's in there, isn't he?" said Beefer. "I got Fs on every homework assignment

this week, and I'm pretty sure it's because of the brain injury he gave me."

"You're probably fine," I said. "Quick, how many pasta salads am I holding up?"

"What are you even *talking* about?" he said, shoving me aside.

"Come on, Beefer, you don't need to do that. Let's go to the vending machine. I'll buy you some Funchos Flavor—"

Beefer threw open my locker with a clang. Inside was my Cretaceous hamster habitat. But there was no sign of Hamstersaurus Rex.

Beefer looked around, confused and angry (his only emotions?). "You made a dinosaur playland in your locker?" he said with disgust.

"Yep," I said. "I'm probably a dumb baby."

"Ha! Only a *dumb baby* would do something like . . . ," said Beefer trailing off, annoyed that I'd beaten him to it. "Sam, if you're lying to me about the hamster, things aren't going to go so well for you . . ."

We stared at each other for a moment. I gulped.

"What I mean is: I'm going to beat you up," explained Beefer.

"Yeah, no, I definitely got that," I said.

"Good," said Beefer, poking me hard in the chest. Then he pointed to his waist, mouthed the words "clear belt," and turned to walk away.

"Seriously, Beefer," I said, "I have no idea where Hamstersaurus Rex is."

And I didn't.

Rembrandt!

CHAPTER 10

I WORRIED ABOUT the little guy all night. But the next morning, Hamstersaurus Rex was back in my locker like nothing had happened. I guessed he just liked to come and go as he pleased. Who was I to stop him?

Now he was snoring quietly, snuggled up next to a purple allosaurus. (Honestly, it was allo-dorable.) I transferred him to my shirt pocket and carried him with me throughout the school day.

My plan was working. Each morning, I secretly stuffed five times the normal amount of food into my lunch box. At lunch, Hamstersaurus Rex gobbled it all down. I kept him fed, and he was a happy little mutant. When school let out, I returned him to his dino habitat for the night. He liked to wrestle the pteranodons and bite the tails off the ankylosaurs.

The next day I would do it all over again.

In history, we learned more about Pilgrims. (Apparently they wore funny hats?) Geometry was triangle city. In science, we read about the discovery of penicillin. Long story short: some guy called Alexander Fleming ate a piece of mold and he wasn't sick anymore? Gross. Anyway, I failed a quiz about it, so don't ask me. Science Night was also mentioned a few times, and I made a note to myself to figure out what it was. Then I made another note to remember that note. In gym we did strange, old-fashioned exercises that nobody seemed to understand. Occasionally, I saw Martha Cherie stalking the halls with purpose, scribbling notes in her Hamstersaurus notebook. Sometimes I saw Beefer looking for Hamstersaurus Rex, too. Despite his claims, he wasn't much of a "Sunblock Holmes," though. He kept checking every toilet in the school, like he thought hamsters could breathe underwater.

I spent most of my time drawing of pictures of Hamstersaurus Rex in different (totally awesome) scenarios. I drew him as a space pirate, as

an old-timey pharmacist, and as a practitioner of savate, the art of French kickboxing. Once, Dylan

caught me sketching a picture of the little guy riding a rocket sled through the desert.

"So why does he have fangs and a tail?" asked Dylan, stroking her chin.

"Huh? What? I don't know," I said. "Why did Rembrandt paint pictures of dolphins playing poker?"

"Um, I don't think he did."

"Artistic license," I said, crumpling up the picture. The more suspicious Dylan got, the guiltier I felt.

Other than that, it was smooth sailing for Sam Gibbs and Hamstersaurus Rex for more than a whole week. Then came the olive tapenade.

"Mom," I said, looking in our fridge before school. "What *is* olive tapenade?"

"It's a spread for sandwiches," she yelled from her office upstairs. She was on her laptop paying bills.

"Like peanut butter?" I yelled back. We were all out of peanut butter.

"For sandwiches," she yelled again, distracted.

I shrugged and began slathering it on slices of bread for my lunch. I made five olive tapenade and jelly sandwiches (with extra olive tapenade). One for me and four for Hamstersaurus Rex.

When I got to school, I found a crowd of kids around my locker. Not a good sign.

"Hey, everybody," I said. "Have I suddenly become popular?"

"Sam, you drew a picture of me where my ears were the size and approximate shape of oven mitts," said Julie Bailey, frowning.

"Right," I said. So I hadn't suddenly become popular.

"Julie and I were just talking about the rash of locker break-ins," said Omar Powell, whose locker was right next to mine. "Mine got hit for the second time this week. *Somebody* stole a whole twenty-seven pack of Mint-Caramel Choconobs." He squinted at me, perhaps recalling the jumping-desk incident.

"I had some Funchos Classic Italian Cheddar-and-Mayo Flavor-Wedges in my locker," said Julie. "Now they're all gone." She held up a bag that had been shredded in a very familiar way.

I opened my own locker an inch and quickly

slammed it shut. "Oh, man," I said. "Me too. I had some food in my locker that *also* got eaten! Hmm. You know who loves junk food *and* committing felonies?" I glanced down the hallway toward Beefer Vanderkoff. He was reading *Pustule* magazine's annual double-sized "Werewolf Issue." Julie and Omar looked at one another. Beefer stealing Flavor-Wedges? It made sense. . . .

"I have another theory," said Martha Cherie, startling us all. How did she just appear out of nowhere like that?

Martha used a pair of tweezers to take Julie Bailey's Funchos bag. Then she produced the frayed solar system string that I'd seen before. She examined them both very closely, with a large magnifying glass.

"Just as I suspected. The same creature gnawed

both. The tooth prints are a match," said Martha. "Hamstersaurus Rex is still in the school. Probably somewhere in this general vicinity." She began to unroll a spool of yellow police tape.

"Wait, can I see that for a second?" I said, taking the bag and the magnifying glass from her. I pretended to inspect it myself. "You know, Martha, I could be wrong, but don't the teeth that made *these* bite marks seem a little sharper than the ones that gnawed through the string? Whatever ripped into this Funchos bag had little dinosaur fangs. Er, so to speak."

"Hmm," said Martha, inspecting the bag again. "Yeah, I see what you're saying. They're *similar* but not identical. I had *no idea* you were interested in rodent dental forensics, Sam."

"It's always been a hobby," I said.

"You two deserve each other," said Omar, shaking his head.

"They do not," said Beefer Vanderkoff, who'd shoved his way forward. Omar and Julie looked at each other and left.

"Very plump greetings," I said. "I am Sam's

identical cousin, Jarmo. From Fin—"

"Shut it," he said, shoving me out of the way. "Hey, Martha, did you know that Sam has a little baby dinosaur playland in his locker? What a dumb stupid idiot, right?"

"'Dumb stupid idiot' is redundant," said Martha, now scribbling furiously in her hamster notebook. "You can just say 'idiot.'"

"Ha-ha. Yeah. Re-*dumb*-dent. Nice one, Martha," said Beefer.

And then he just stood there—for ten awkward seconds—staring at his feet and silently mouthing words like he was rehearsing something. Beefer Vanderkoff seemed to be displaying an emotion that was neither confusion nor anger. Was the most menacing bully at Horace Hotwater Middle School *nervous*?

When Beefer finally spoke again, his voice was an octave higher. "Yeah, so, anyway, there's this new movie coming out this week, and it's called *Wolfsplosion IV*. And it's all about these werewolves that keep exploding, but nobody can figure out why. In *Wolfsplosion I* and *II* it was because of a

ghost. In *Wolfsplosion III* it was aliens. Who knows why it's happening this time. But *IV* is supposed to be the best in the series. *Pustule* called it the 'Citizen Kane of exploding werewolf movies.'"

"Hmm," said Martha. She didn't look up from her notebook.

"Yeah, so, anyway maybe we could . . . go see it?" said Beefer. "Together."

"Sorry, but I'm only interested in watching movies that have been deemed appropriate for my age range by the Motion Picture Association of America," said Martha. "That means a G-rating or lower."

"Oh," said Beefer. "Well, we don't have to go to a movie. Do you want to come over to my house and watch my pet boa constrictor eat a live rat?"

"No, thanks," said Martha, still taking notes.

"Okay," said Beefer, looking down at the ground. "Then bye, I guess."

Martha ignored him as he slunk off. The whole thing was so painful I almost pitied the guy. Almost.

"Nice work on this, Sam," said Martha, holding up the Flavor-Wedges bag. "Maybe one day you could make Junior Deputy Hamster Monitor."

"Fingers crossed," I said.

"For the record," said Martha, "I still think Hamstersaurus Rex is around here somewhere. But now it looks like there's some sort of new lizard-y creature on the loose, too."

If only she knew they were one and the same. "I guess it's a lizard that's addicted to junk food," I said. "This school keeps getting weirder and weirder."

"Funchos Flavor-Wedges. Mint-Caramel Choconobs," said Martha, making notes. "What was eaten out of your locker?"

"My locker? Nothi— Oh, right. Just some Cheez Wallets."

"Very interesting," said Martha. "All those products are made by SmilesCorp."

"Huh. Just like Coach Weekes's health supplements," I said without thinking. "I mean, probably just a coincidence."

"Probably," said Martha, chewing the end of her pencil. "We can compare notes on the case when we go to the ADM."

"The ADM?"

"The Antique Doll Museum, silly!" said Martha with an eerie giggle.

"Sure. Right. The Antique Doll Museum," I said, my heart sinking. "A place that I promised to go."

The bell rang, and Martha dashed off toward

homeroom without another word. Once I was alone, I opened my locker again. Hammie Rex stared back at me with wide eyes. He looked worried.

"That was a close one, pal," I said as I transferred him to my pocket. "Look, you *can't* keep stealing food from other people's lockers. Low profile, remember?"

He growled.

"I promise I'll keep you fed, little buddy," I said. "Don't you worry."

Reality wasn't so simple, though. At lunch, I snuck off—Dylan had come to expect it—and hid behind my favorite stack of chairs. I pulled out one of the sandwiches and shoved it into my pocket for Hammie Rex to eat. He took one bite and his eyes crossed.

"What's wrong?"

Hamstersaurus Rex spat the sandwich out. It flew ten feet and stuck to a mural of anthropomorphic letters eating vegetables. The little guy shuddered.

"That's rude!" I whispered. "I slaved over a

room-temperature kitchen counter for three minutes on that sandwich. What are you, some kind of picky eater now?"

He was trying to wipe the taste off his tongue, but his stumpy little paws were too short to reach. He gave up and used his back feet.

"Mmm, it's good. See?" I took a bite of one of the sandwiches and gagged. It turns out, olive tapenade isn't that much like peanut butter after all. I spit my own sandwich out and wiped my own tongue with my hands. Hamstersaurus Rex stared pitifully. His stomach gave a warning rumble.

So I went through the cafeteria line. "Hi," I said.

"You again," said Judy.

"Yep. Can I have four helpings of shepherd's pie, please?"

"*Four* helpings?"

"Actually, make that five." I'd forgotten that I needed to eat, too.

She crossed her arms and scowled at me. "This is some kind of joke, isn't it?" she said. "I've worked here for twenty-seven years and *nobody*

has *ever* asked for seconds of shepherd's pie. It comes out of a fifty-gallon drum we keep in the parking lot, you know."

"I'm a shepherd's pie fanatic!" I said. "Every time the cafeteria serves shepherd's pie, it feels like a national holiday to me."

"Then why haven't you ever eaten it before?"

"Because . . . absence makes the heart grow fonder?" I said.

"I will serve you *one* helping of shepherd's pie," said Judy. "And that's all." And she took a ladle, dipped it into the beefy reddish slop, and dumped it onto my tray.

I dashed off. Alone, once again, I spooned half of the shepherd's pie into my pocket. "Sorry, pal," I said to Hamstersaurus Rex. "Not ideal, but we're going to have to split this."

He gobbled it down and then whined for more. He blinked his little eyes. His lip quivered. He looked like he was going to cry. Can hamsters cry? Can dinosaurs cry?

"Okay, fine," I said. And I spooned him the other half. Still, it wasn't enough. He squeaked with hunger. I'd never heard him squeak before.

"You want another OT and J?" I asked. "That stands for 'olive tapenade and jelly.'" He hissed at me and stuck his tongue out.

So, it was back through the cafeteria line for me. Lunch was almost over, so it was just Judy now.

"Don't even *think* about asking for more shepherd's pie," she said, pointing to the chafing dish in front of her. It was practically empty.

"I'd like a roll," I said. "Just a plain old roll." I tried to smile.

Judy gritted her teeth and picked one up with her tongs.

"You know, actually," I said, trying to sound casual, "could you make that fifteen rolls?"

"No!" said Judy, putting the roll back. "I hate it when you kids waste food!"

I tried to persuade her that I didn't intend to waste anything. Meanwhile, I somehow failed to notice that Hamstersaurus Rex was no longer in my shirt pocket.

". . . To sum up," said Judy, pointing her tongs at me menacingly, "I don't know what you're up to, young man, but I don't find it funny at all!"

At that moment, I saw Hamstersaurus Rex right behind her. He was sitting next to a brand-new chafing dish full of shepherd's pie, fresh from the oven (or wherever they heat the stuff up to body temperature). He was licking his little dino chops.

"Oh no!" I said without thinking.

"What?" said Judy.

If she turned around she would see Hamstersaurus Rex two feet behind her. It was distraction time.

"Hey!" I said. "Look at *this*!" I began to do an impromptu tap dance across the cafeteria floor.

TAP
TAP
TAP
TAP!!!

Judy stared at me with wide eyes, utterly baffled. Behind her, Hammie Rex dove headfirst into the chafing dish full of shepherd's pie.

"Whaddya think?" I said as I frantically danced, trying to hold her attention. "No formal training. Pretty good, right?"

"I have *no idea* what you're doing," said Judy. "But if you *keep* doing it I'm going to call the school psychologist."

"Oh, it's just a little soft-shoe!" I wildly spun and tapped my feet and flailed my hands around. I have no idea how to tap-dance, but I gave it my all.

"Look, I'm going to be perfectly honest, son," said Judy, cocking her head. "The dance isn't great."

Hamstersaurus Rex had devoured half a chafing dish of shepherd's pie now. He was still going.

"Oh yeah?" I said. "But what about this?" I started jumping wildly, trying (and failing) to touch my toes. If anything this new move seemed to disturb Judy even more.

"That's worse," she said. "Your hand work is sloppy. Your rhythm is weak. Honestly, you're all over the place. And if you want to tap dance, you need tap shoes."

Hamstersaurus Rex sat in an empty chafing dish now. He burped. His furry belly was the size of a tennis ball. He sluggishly climbed out and dropped to the floor.

"Oh well," I said to Judy. "Maybe my dream of becoming a dancer is unrealistic, after all. Goodbye!" I turned on my heel and left, passing a few baffled classmates.

"Wait. Don't give up that easily, kid," Judy called after me. "*Believe* in yourself!"

I rounded a corner, and Hammie Rex stood on the ground before me. He held up his stumpy little arms like he wanted to be carried. I grabbed him and stuffed him back in my pocket. He was so full of shepherd's pie, he barely fit.

"Not cool," I said.

He stared up at me and blinked.

"Okay, it was actually kind of awesome," I admitted. "But don't do it again, okay."

The lunch bell rang.

"Sam, what happened?" asked Dylan as we filed out of the cafeteria toward gym class. "You disappeared yet again. What's going on, dude?"

"Sorry, I—I forgot something," I said. I could tell she was hurt. At this point I should have told her everything, but . . . I knew how disappointed she'd be. Turns out, the longer you tell a lie, the harder it is to get out of. "Hey, I know I've been all over the place recently," I said, changing the subject, "but what have you been up to?"

"Training," she said.

"Training? For what?"

"For the Little Mister or Miss Muscles Competition," said Dylan. "It's today."

CHAPTER 11

COACH WEEKES STOOD in the gym with his arms crossed. Martha Cherie was beside him holding a clipboard.

"All right, line up, you *kids!*" bellowed Coach Weekes, really drawing out the last word. "Believe me, if I *could* call all of you 'maggots' I *would,* but the school hand-book makes it very clear that I cannot. Got it?"

Nobody said anything as we formed a line.

Coach Weekes looked us up and down and then shook his head in disgust. "Your generation has been pampered by video games and seat belts and such. When I was a kid, the seat belt just went across the lap. No shoulder strap! And the only video games we had were crappy. Terrible graphics. You'd die three times and have to start all over again. No saves! But still we played them all day, anyway. And we didn't complain!"

We stared at Coach Weekes, confused.

"What are you getting at, Coach?" said Dylan.

"My point, D'Amato, is that when I was young, everything was harder and also better! That's why I've decided to bring back Little Mister or Miss Muscles. In the year 1983—probably the peak of human civilization—we knew what a real test of physical fitness was. We didn't toss little flying saucers around at stuff and call it a sport."

"The first disc golf game was played in 1926," said Dylan, crossing her arms, "in Bladworth, Saskatchewan."

"Yeah, right. You just made that up, D'Amato.

You and I both know 'Saskatchewan' isn't a real place," said Coach Weekes. "Anyway, zip it. It's time for Little Mister or Miss Muscles. The first feat in this legendary competition is Knuckle-ups. A true test of arm-al and shoulder-al strength. Whoever does the most in thirty seconds wins. I earned this"—he held up his trophy, barely recognizable since it had been taped back together—"by doing eighteen knuckle-ups."

I raised my hand. "Um, what if, hypothetically, someone couldn't do any knuckle-ups at all?"

"Then that would be completely humiliating and everyone would probably laugh at that person," said Coach Weekes. "Hypothetically."

"Great," I said.

I felt Hamstersaurus Rex stir. He poked his head out of my pocket and growled in Coach Weekes's direction. It was like he could sense when someone was making fun of me.

"Easy, pal," I whispered as I shoved him back down. "If you eat him, I'll probably have to retake this stupid class."

Coach Weekes blew his whistle. "You ready

with that clipboard, Cherie?" he said.

Martha nodded and held it up. "It's the Rentzler 'Executive' model (A SmilesCorp Product™). The choice of scorekeepers everywhere."

"Hang on," said Dylan. "Martha doesn't have to participate?"

"My parents arranged for me to do my Little Mister or Miss Muscles in advance," said Martha matter-of-factly. "The college admissions process is very competitive these days, and they figured that any little bit might help."

"Of course that's what happened," said Dylan, gritting her teeth.

Coach Weekes shrugged. "Enough chitter-chatter. On your knuckles, D'Amato! Get ready! Get set! Go!"

Dylan did twenty-one knuckle-ups. Martha jotted it down. Coach Weekes could barely believe it.

"Got to get this stopwatch checked," he grumbled, holding it up to his ear. "All right, you're next, Choi. You don't want to play disc golf for the rest of the year, do you? So let's see you do twenty-two!"

Jimmy Choi dropped to his knuckles. And so,

one by one, each of the students in our class did as many as they could. I gradually shifted myself down the line until I was standing at the end, on the far side of Wilbur Weber. I was pretty sure I couldn't do a single knuckle-up. I hoped Wilbur wouldn't be able to do one, either. If there were two of us in a row, maybe I wouldn't look quite so pathetic. Maybe.

"Look alive, Weber. You're up," said Coach Weekes. Now only Wilbur and I remained. According to Martha's count, Dylan was still in the lead by four.

"On your knuckles, son!" said Coach Weekes. "Go!"

Wilbur Weber flopped on the ground and laid there, motionless, just as I had wished. For nearly half a minute the class stared at him in uncomfortable silence.

Coach Weekes sighed. I wondered if Wilbur had actually fallen asleep. But somehow, one second before time was up, he grunted and did a single, perfect knuckle-up.

"What?" I cried. "Come *on!*"

Everyone looked at me.

"I mean, good job, Wilbur," I said. "Way to go, buddy. Perseverance."

He shrugged.

"It's showtime, Gibbs," said Coach Weekes. "Let's see what those little noodle arms can do. And when I say 'noodle arms,' as per the school handbook, I don't mean that as an insult. I love noodles. I eat 'em with ketchup. Anyway, on your knuckles."

"I think I can save us all some time," I said. "Just mark me down for a zero, Martha. Thanks."

"Nope," said Coach Weekes. "On your knuckles."

"Really?"

He nodded. I laid on the ground—careful not to squish Hamstersaurus Rex in my breast pocket. I could hear the other kids starting to snicker and whisper among themselves.

"Get set. Go!" cried Coach Weekes.

I took a deep breath and tried to mentally prepare myself for thirty seconds of humiliation. But instead a funny thing happened: I did a knuckle-up. Then I did another. And another. I was doing knuckle-ups. They were so easy!

I realized this was because Hamstersaurus Rex was the one actually doing all the work. Inside my pocket, the little guy was jumping up and down, bouncing me right off the ground. Man, he really was as strong as a dinosaur! The other kids weren't laughing anymore. They had fallen silent.

"Stop!" cried Coach Weekes, punching his watch.

I sat up and smiled. I'd barely broken a sweat. Everyone in the class was staring at me, wide-eyed. Especially Coach Weekes.

"Forty-five," said Martha.

At that, the class let out a cheer. Everyone except Beefer, of course.

"That's a hundred and fourteen percent more knuckle-ups than Dylan," Martha added.

"How did you do forty-five knuckle-ups?"

asked Coach Gibbs, scratching his head.

"Beginner's luck?" I said with a shrug.

"Wow, Sam. I didn't know you had that kind of knuckle power," said Dylan, slapping me on the back. She smiled, but it looked a little forced.

"All right, that means Gibbs is in first place. D'Amato is second. And then after her is McCoy."

While nobody was watching, I gave Hamster-saurus Rex a quick belly rub. He closed his eyes and kicked his back foot.

"Now it's on to the second Little Mister or Miss Muscles fitness feat: the fabled Rod Bend," said Coach Weekes. "Everybody grab one of these." He indicated a plastic barrel full of shiny metal rods, each a quarter-inch thick. We all took one.

"Hold your metal rod like so," said Coach Weekes, grabbing it by both ends. "And bend it as far as you can in thirty seconds. Now, watch and learn!"

Coach Weekes took a deep breath and then started. He quivered and strained and his mustache fluttered like a frightened bird. With a high-pitched shriek he managed to bend his metal rod ever so slightly. Time was up. Panting, Weekes took a protractor from Martha and measured the angle of the bend. "One hundred sixty-one degrees. Would have been better, but I recently hurt both my arms saving an old woman from drowning. When I won Little Mister Muscles back in 1983, I did a hundred and forty-five degrees. Now *that* was an epic bend. . . ."

He looked at us like he was expecting someone to ask for the whole story. Nobody did.

"All right. Fine, then." Coach Weekes looked at his stopwatch. "Rods up, everybody. On your mark. Get set. Bend!"

We all attempted to bend our rods. Mine wouldn't move at all. Dylan was bending hers a little. Wilbur Weber was using his to clean inside his ear. Nobody was watching, so I whispered to Hamstersaurus Rex. "Um, if there's any way you can handle this one, there's another belly rub in it for you. Possibly a behind-the-ear scratch."

The little guy seemed to understand. He popped his head out of my pocket, opened his jaws wide, and bit down hard on the middle of the rod. The force of his dino chomp practically folded the thing in half! I held the two ends until the time was up.

Coach Weekes blew his whistle. "Stop bend-

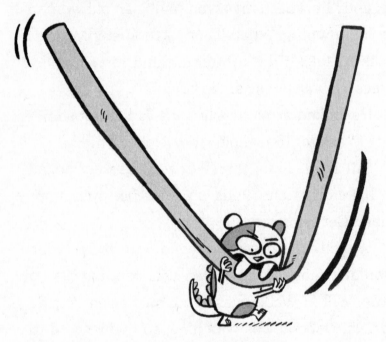

ing! Rods down, people! Rods down!"

One by one, he inspected our metal rods and measured the angle with his protractor. Martha recorded the results. He whistled when he saw mine.

"Fifteen degrees," he said, after measuring and

remeasuring. He looked at me with genuine suspicion. "How'd you manage that, Gibbs?"

"I've been bending stuff around the house for practice," I said. "I was skeptical at first, but now I feel like Little Mister or Miss Muscles is more than just a bunch of weirdly outdated, possibly dangerous fitness tests for kids. It's about giving it your all and seeing if you really have what it takes to be number one. It's about becoming a champion."

"Gibbs, honestly that's . . . that's beautiful," said Coach Weekes. He wiped a tear from the corner of his eye. "Write that down, Cherie."

Martha started writing.

"Sam, I thought you forgot about Little Mister or Miss Muscles," said Dylan.

I was about to reply, but Coach Weekes interrupted. "You're just sore 'cause he's beating you, D'Amato! For the Rod Bend we have Gibbs coming in first. Again D'Amato in the number two spot. And in third place we have, ugh, Vanderkoff, who is automatically disqualified because he broke my trophy the other day."

"Whatever," said Beefer. "This class is dumb

and I hate everyone. Except, uh . . ." He glanced at Martha. She kept on scribbling on her clipboard. Beefer kicked his metal rod across the floor of the gym with a loud clang.

"Never disrespect the Rod Bend, Vanderkoff," said Coach Weekes. "Principal Truitt's office *now*."

Beefer shrugged. He probably spent more time in the principal's office than the principal did.

"Cherie," said Coach Weekes to Martha. "Escort Vanderkoff to make sure he actually gets there. Last time I sent him on his own, he somehow managed to start a fire in the water fountain."

Martha raised her hand. "May I ask a question?"

Coach Weekes sighed. "No, temporarily leaving class won't affect your attendance record."

Dylan rolled her eyes. If eye rolls had been part of the competition, she would have won easily. Martha nodded and handed the Rentzler Executive to Omar to keep score. Then she and Beefer—who seemed perfectly happy with his punishment now that it involved Martha—left together.

"All right, this is the final portion of the competition," said Coach Weekes. "It all comes down to this, kids. Can you feel the electricity?"

Nobody could. I turned my back to the other kids and gave Hamstersaurus Rex a quick round of victory scratches in my pocket. It was the least I could do.

"Welcome to the Sixty-Foot Sandbag Drag," said Coach Weekes, waving dramatically. On the floor of the gym, sitting at a starting line, was a sandbag the size of a pillow. It had a heavy rope tied around it.

"Competitors drag the sandbag a distance of sixty feet," said Coach Weekes, "to there." He pointed to a finish line on the other side of the gym. "Whoever does it the fastest wins."

"This is literally the dumbest thing I've ever heard of," said Dylan.

"Quiet, D'Amato," said Coach Weekes. "On your mark!"

Dylan walked to the starting line, rolling her shoulders.

"Get set!"

Dylan spat on her palms, grabbed the end of the rope, and threw it over her shoulder. She nodded to Coach Weekes.

"Go!" he cried.

Dylan strained and dragged the bag across the floor at a slow jog. I could see the effort in her face as she crossed the finish line.

"Ten-point-four seconds!" called out Coach Weekes, looking at his stopwatch. "Not bad for having the wind at your back."

"We're inside," said Dylan, wiping the sweat from her brow. "There isn't any wind."

"It was the air conditioning then," said Coach Weekes.

The Sixty-Foot Sandbag Drag looked hard. The sandbag itself was massive. I doubted I could move it an inch, much less sixty whole feet. Still, by the time it was my turn, I was feeling pretty confident.

"I think you know what to do, amigo," I whispered to Hammie Rex. He looked me square in the eyes and burped. That's Hamstersaurus Rex for "we're on the same page." Martha and Beefer were gone, so I decided I could risk it. I opened my pocket, and he jumped out and scurried across the floor of the gym.

I walked to the starting line and grabbed the rope. Wow, even the rope was heavy.

"You can do this, Gibbs," said Coach Weekes. "Sure, when this class period started, I thought you were pathetic. A physically weak specimen who likes drawing little pictures more than doing important stuff, like sports. But you proved me wrong by winning two out of three Little Mister or Miss Muscles events. Now I see that you've got the fire in your guts. You've got the champion's will." He leaned in close and whispered, "Gibbs, you have the spirit of the Velvet Shark."

"No," I said, thumping my chest. "I've got the spirit of the Dinosaur Hamster!"

"I don't get it, but I love it!" said Coach Weekes, slapping me on the back. "All right. On your mark, Gibbs. Get set. Go!"

I pulled the rope. The sandbag wouldn't budge. I gritted my teeth and strained with my whole body. At last, the bag shifted. I started to walk. Then run. Faster and faster, the sandbag trailing behind me. Everyone cheered me on.

It only got weird when the sandbag actually

sped up and passed me.

"Hey, not so fast!" I said. "We've got to make this look convincing."

The bag slowed just in time for me to pass it and cross the finish line.

Coach Weekes blew his whistle. "Seven-point-seven seconds!" he cried, staring at his watch. "Seven-point-seven seconds! Unbelievable! Ladies and gentlemen, we have a new Little Mister or Miss Muscles!"

The class exploded in applause. People patted me on the back and shook my hand. I smiled. It was the nicest anyone had been since seeing their Sam Gibbs caricatures.

"Congratulations, Sam," said Dylan, giving me a bear hug. "If it wasn't me, I'm glad it was you who won."

"I win a lot of awards for participation," said Wilbur Weber to no one in particular.

"You keep this up, Gibbs," said Coach Weekes, beaming as he shook my hand, "and you could be the next *me*!"

It was a terrifying thought but not enough to

bring down my mood. Yes, I'll admit that it felt pretty good to be crowned the new Little Mister or Miss Muscles. I poked my index finger into my pocket and gave Hamstersaurus Rex the world's smallest high five.

CHAPTER 12

MY TRIUMPH WAS short-lived. After PE but before math, I somehow found myself in the second-floor boys' bathroom, alone yet again with Beefer Vanderkoff. I guess it's true what they say: those who forget history are doomed to repeat it.

"We've got to stop meeting like this," I said with a forced laugh.

Beefer wasn't smiling. "I heard you won that dumb Muscles thing while I was chilling in the principal's office," he said. "Big deal, Sam." He'd put himself between me and the door now. Running for my life was out.

"Yeah, I guess the adrenaline just took over," I

said. "You know what that's like. From when you head-butt rocks or take lunch money from the weak or whatever."

"You may have all of them fooled," said Beefer. "But I know something's up."

"Uh," I said. Not the greatest comeback. Did he know that Hamstersaurus Rex was in my shirt pocket at that very moment?

"I see what you're doing," said Beefer, "trying to move in and steal Martha Cherie from me?"

"What?"

"On the way to the principal's office, she told me how much you wanted to go the doll museum with her."

"But I don't!"

"She said you two are even going to ride one of those dumb double bicycles."

"Okay, yes that's happening, but it's not what it sounds like. I don't, you know, *like* Martha like that."

"Oh, so you're just playing games, huh? You don't care if you break her heart?" said Beefer, looking, if possible, angrier than he ever had before.

"I'm not. I mean—"

"And now I look like a fool," said Beefer. "Just like when you showed everybody that picture you drew of me."

"It was nothing personal. I was just trying to learn how to do caricatures! And they weren't stink lines, they were *motion* lines—"

"You want to take something from me that I care about, then I'm going to take something *you* care about: that dumb gerbil. That's right. I know *exactly* where he is. . . ."

"You do?"

"Uh-huh," said Beefer, nodding. "He's living in the computer lab, eating electricity to survive."

It occurred to me that Beefer really didn't know very much about hamsters.

"And when I catch him there," he continued, "POW!" Beefer slammed his fist into his palm.

I felt Hamstersaurus Rex tense up inside my pocket. He sensed I was in danger, and he wanted to defend me. I mentally tried to will him to stay still.

"But first," said Beefer, grabbing me by the

collar and marching me toward one of the bath-room stalls, "I'm going to show you the new and improved KiBeVaUl-Swi."

"The what?" I said. "Oh, right."

"Like any good innovator I'm always trying to improve my product," said Beefer. "Pancake batter in the toilet bowl was a good idea. But this is better." He hefted a twenty-pound bag of fast-drying, powdered cement and gave me a sickening smile.

"Come on, Beefer. You can't be serious."

Beefer flushed the toilet and emptied the bag into the bowl. I watched as the cement powder dissolved and the water slowly thickened into a churning gray goop.

"Oh, I'm serious," said Beefer. "A thousand years from now, when people hear the name Vanderkoff, I want them to remember a true pioneer in the field of toilet-based bullying."

"Please. Don't put my head in there, it's—"

Beefer punched me in the stomach, and I doubled over, gasping for air.

"What's that, Sam?" he said, yanking me toward the toilet. "Can't hear you, buddy. Were you about to say something?"

I opened my mouth and then came the loudest sound I've ever heard—even louder than one of my mom's sneezes! It was a booming roar, so powerful that it shattered one of the bathroom mirrors. But the noise hadn't come from me—

it had come from Hamstersaurus Rex!

Beefer's smug, ugly face instantly became a mask of terror. He stumbled backward and tripped. To catch his balance, he put his foot right into the cement-filled toilet.

With a squeal—well, he looked like he was squealing; I couldn't really tell because my ears were still ringing from Hammie Rex's roar—he realized his foot was stuck in the goop.

Now Beefer frantically tried to pull his foot out to get away from me. He yanked once, twice. But the cement was hardening quickly, and the toilet wouldn't release its grip. With one final pull, Beefer broke the toilet right off the wall. He flew backward and somehow—to this day, I'm not quite sure how—he managed to fall so that his head landed inside a urinal.

Beefer's left foot was still stuck in the hardened cement bowl of the now-liberated toilet; his head was wedged tightly inside the urinal.

I stared at him for a minute, unsure what to do. Water gushed from the broken pipe, spilling onto the floor of the bathroom.

"Do you need help?" I said at last.

At this Beefer shrieked and began to quake with fear. It was like he thought I was going to murder him or something. In his wild flailing, he somehow swung his heavy toilet foot up and broke the handle off the urinal. This started a continuous flush pouring over his the top of his head.

I heard the sound of the door. Other boys from my class stood in the doorway now.

"Holy crap," said Omar Powell. "Sam beat up Beefer."

I rushed past him out of the bathroom. Inside my pocket, I heard something that sounded a lot like mutant dino-hamster laughter.

CHAPTER 13

A GOOD DAY for me might involve getting an extra piece of cinnamon toast at breakfast. Maybe buying a new pair of shoelaces. But winning a class-wide fitness competition *and* getting revenge on the bully who has tormented me for years? That was a whole different category of good day for Sam Gibbs.

It eventually took four custodians and the school nurse to extricate Beefer from his predicament. (They had to use the Jaws of Life to break the urinal off his head!) But he wasn't rescued before every single boy (and most of the girls) at Horace Hotwater Middle School paid a visit to the second-floor boys' bathroom to witness the humiliation of Beefer Vanderkoff. Some of them took pictures.

I came to school the next morning feeling like a king. When I got there, a crowd of students stood around my locker. Everyone wanted to talk to me.

"Nice work, Sam," said Jimmy Choi, shaking my hand. "I've hated Beefer ever since kindergarten, when he broke all my crayons."

"It was nothing," I said.

"I'm never giving another cent of lunch money to that guy," said Omar Powell. "I knew he wasn't really a karate master."

"Hey, maybe you earn the clear belt for eating corn chips?" I said.

And everyone laughed. Seriously. They *laughed*. At one of *my* jokes!

"Sam, can you teach me how to do more knuckle-ups?" said Drew McCoy.

"Sure, no problem," I said. "It's all about proper form."

"Any plans this weekend, Sam?" asked Julie Bailey, smiling brightly.

"Just kind of playing it by ear," I said. "Um, speaking of ears, you're not still mad about the caricature?"

"No way! That's ancient history. Besides, we can call it even. In first grade I told everyone that you, um, had an accident."

"Wait, that was you?" I said. So Dylan *hadn't* spilled the beans about that one. Maybe she wasn't as big of a blabbermouth as I thought.

"Anyway, Sam," said Julie, "if you're free Saturday maybe—"

"Maybe you could come over and see my snails," said Wilbur Weber, edging her out.

"Yeah, maybe, Wilbur," I said. "You know, I actually think I have something on Saturday. And also on Sunday. But—"

"I like to smear glue all over my face and then peel it off like skin!" said Jared Kopernik.

"Uh . . . cool, Jared," I said.

"Hey, speak of the devil," said Omar.

Down the hall I saw Beefer Vanderkoff, eyes on the ground, slinking toward his locker. As he passed, other kids whispered and pointed.

Somehow, Beefer looked six inches shorter than he had yesterday.

Someone in the crowd called out, "What's up, Toilet Foot?"

Beefer flinched but didn't respond.

Someone else yelled, "Nah, he goes by Urinal Head now!"

Toilet Foot? Urinal Head? In my opinion, they were both great nicknames for Beefer. Maybe a good compromise would be "Toilet-Urinal Foot-Head"? My mom says it's wrong to take pleasure in the misfortunes of others, but I will admit, I giggled. For five minutes straight.

The bell rang, and I waited for the crowd to disperse before I opened my locker.

Hammie Rex was inside looking just as happy as I felt. He was wagging his tail and kicking sand all over the place.

"All aboard," I said, holding my shirt pocket open.

With a growl, Hamstersaurus Rex leaped into the air, did a flip, and landed in my pocket.

"Hamsterrific!" I said.

Class was a breeze. I doodled all morning, mostly pictures of a fifty-foot-tall Hamstersaurus Rex stomping on a regular-sized Beefer. I even threw caution to the wind and let Hamstersaurus Rex  sneak a peek at my artwork. He approved (burped). Mr. Copeland surprised me once by calling on me in class. He expected that I wouldn't know the answer. And I certainly didn't. But I happened to guess "Wampanoag Confederacy," which turned out to be correct. Mr. Copeland was very impressed. I did get a few more bad grades in science and again somebody mentioned something about Science Night, but I wasn't really sweating it. Nothing could bring me down.

"Way to finally stand up to Beefer," said Dylan at lunch.

"Please. No need to call me a hero. I'm just a regular guy who was pushed too far," I said, chewing my ham and cheese sandwich.

"I didn't call you a hero," said Dylan. "So I guess that means you're not worried at all?"

"Worried about what?"

"This," said Dylan. She slid a poorly photocopied note across the table. It read:

COME TO THE MUNKEY BARS AT RESESS TO LEARN SAM GIBBSE'S TERRIBAL SECRIT.

WARNING THIS NOTE IS ALSO SECRIT!!! DO NOT TELL ANY BODY ESPESHALLY SAM!!!

SINCERELY, ANONIMUS

ANONIMUS, huh? It looked like it had been written by a preschooler. That's how I knew it was Beefer.

"He put these in everyone's lockers," said Dylan. "What do you think he's up to?"

"No idea," I said. "But I guess I'm going to find out."

"You *don't* have one, do you, Sam?"

"One what?"

"A secret."

I squirmed, feeling guilty. "What? No way. I'm an open book."

Her face looked pained. "If you need help, Sam, I could help you. Just like in preschool when you had the sand pail stuck on your head. We're best friends. That's what we do."

"Look, I already told you, I don't know where Hamstersaurus Rex is!"

"I didn't mention Hamstersaurus Rex," said Dylan.

At recess, a crowd had formed near the monkey bars. They were whispering and joking among themselves. It seemed like people were expecting Beefer to somehow make a bigger fool of himself than he already had. Everyone except Dylan, that is. She stood apart with her arms crossed, her face unreadable.

"Oh no!" said Tina Gomez, feigning fear as I approached. "It's Sam 'Terribal Secrit' Gibbs."

"I'll admit it," I said. "I know what the cafeteria shepherd's pie is *really made of.*"

People laughed—for the second time that day—at something I said. Man, I could get used to that!

"Guys, I told all of you not to tell *him!*" came a shrill cry from behind me.

As I turned, the crowd parted to reveal Beefer Vanderkoff. He stared at me wide-eyed, no less terrified than yesterday.

"You've got something to say, Beefer?" I said throwing out my chest. "Say it to my face." My best effort at tough-guy talk. It seemed to impress everyone.

"Yeah, what's the big secret, Urinal Head?" said Tina Gomez to Beefer. "The suspense is killing me."

"I'll tell you, but once I reveal it, you have to promise to protect me from *him*," said Beefer, pointing in my direction. I looked over my shoulder. No, he really did mean me.

"Sure, we promise," said Omar Powell, snickering.

Beefer cleared his throat. "Well, Sam's been acting extra weird lately. Sure, he's always been weird—and also a dumb baby and a total jerk— like when he drew me with the stink lines—"

"Spare us, Beefer. Two years ago, you snipped off one my pigtails. So in my book, *you're* the jerk," said Julie Bailey. "Just get on with it, will you, Toilet Foot?"

Beefer frowned. "First off, I've seen Sam getting all this extra food in the cafeteria and bringing five sandwiches in his lunch box, too."

Beefer had seen that? I guess I'd been less sneaky than I thought. I noticed Dylan looking at me.

"Plus other snacks have been going missing from other people's lockers," said Beefer, "and it wasn't even me who stole them this time!"

"So Sam eats a lot," said Drew McCoy. "You do, too, Beefer. So what?"

"I know, but overeating is, like, *normal* for me," said Beefer.

"The big secret is that Sam likes sandwiches?" said Jimmy Choi. "La-a-aaame."

"No, wait!" said Beefer. "That's just part of it. Think about how all of a sudden Sam wins Little Mister Muscles. How did he do it? Look at him. He's still a puny little nerd!"

The crowd murmured now. It seemed like a few of them were actually starting to consider what Beefer was saying. I tried to look less puny.

"And yesterday, when I was about to stick his head in a toilet full of wet cement," said Beefer, "he *roared* at me."

At this, the crowd went quiet.

"Sam roared at you?" said Dylan.

"Yes!" said Beefer. "It was the scariest sound I've ever heard. No human could make a noise like that. No, it was more like an animal or a—a monster."

Everyone was staring at me now. Some of them

looked uncertain. Unconsciously, my hand went to my shirt pocket. It was empty.

"I know that what I'm about to say is going to sound strange," said Beefer, taking a deep breath, "but please keep an open mind. The world is more complex than—"

"Spit it out, Beefer," said Drew.

"I believe that Sam Gibbs," said Beefer, pausing as he pointed at me dramatically, "is a *werewolf*!"

Everyone turned to stare at Beefer again. Then they all burst out laughing.

"You watch way too many horror movies, dude!" said Omar.

"I think that urinal waterlogged your brain," said Julie Bailey.

"I'm so glad I showed up for this," said Jimmy Choi, hugging Beefer's note.

"No!" cried Beefer. "Think about it: Super strength! Increased appetite! Roaring! It all adds up!"

"Werewolves don't roar," said Tina Gomez. "They howl."

"Sometimes they roar," cried Beefer desperately.

"Aaaaaaaaaooooooooooooooo!" I howled.

Everyone laughed.

"Come on, now he's faking not being a werewolf," cried Beefer. "That's the oldest werewolf trick in the werewolf book! Watch *Wolfsplosion II*, people! I don't get why nobody is taking this seriou—"

At that moment, Beefer's sweatpants fell down around his ankles, revealing his pale legs and a dingy pair of tighty-whities.

The laughter tripled as Beefer struggled (unsuccessfully) to pull them back up.

"This is a conspiracy!" he cried. "Somebody sabotaged my drawstring to make me look like a dummy!" He pulled the string out of his waistband, and sure enough it had been gnawed into two pieces. A flash of orange fur darting behind the slide left me with little doubt as to who had done it. Hamstersaurus Rex had escaped from my pocket to deal a deathblow to Beefer's credibility!

"Hey, Beefer, if you really need to hold up your pants," I said, "you can always use your *clear belt*."

This got another huge laugh.

"He has you all tricked!" cried Beefer. "He was just a regular, smart-mouth dweeb, but now the curse of the wolf is upon him! Beware! None of us are safe!"

"Come on. What am I going to do?" I said. "Eat you?" And I lunged toward Beefer, baring my teeth. He shrieked and ran as fast as he could across the playground and back toward the school. To the delight of the crowd, his pants fell down six or seven times along the way.

My own smile faded as I turned to see that Dylan was peeking behind the slide. Had she seen Hammie Rex, too?

"Dylan, wait!" I cried, running toward her. "You shouldn't—"

"Shouldn't *what*?" said Dylan.

Relief! Hamstersaurus Rex wasn't there.

"You shouldn't, uh, go down this slide," I said. "It . . . has ants on it."

I tried to smile. The bell rang. Recess was over.

"You're not telling me something, Sam," said Dylan. "You *do* have a secret. It's like I don't even know you anymore."

"No, I'm being honest. I—I promise!"

Dylan squinted at me but didn't say anything as she turned and walked back toward the school.

I found Hamstersaurus Rex gnawing on the base of the monkey bars. He didn't understand why I didn't feel like playing.

CHAPTER 14

THAT FRIDAY AFTER school, I placed Hammie Rex into my locker dino-habitat for the weekend.

"You know the drill, little buddy," I said, scratching his scaly spine. "I leave a bunch of extra sandwiches for the next two days, and then I see you bright and early on Monday morning." I unloaded ten PB and Js from my backpack and stacked them in the back of the locker. Hammie Rex gurgled.

Things felt a little safer since Beefer hadn't shown his face at Horace Hotwater for two whole days. Perhaps he feared the "curse of the wolf." Maybe he was just too embarrassed to return. The annoying thing was, I felt kind of guilty about it. Sure his comeuppance had gone a *little* far, but he deserved it. Didn't he? I tried to joke about it with Dylan the day before, but she didn't laugh.

I sighed. "Okay. Don't eat these sandwiches all in one sitting," I said, knowing Hamstersaurus Rex definitely would.

Despite the food, the little guy seemed glum, too. He kicked a toy stegosaurus and made a kind of whining grumble as he stomped around in circles. His eyes looked moist. His tail drooped. He didn't want me to leave.

"That's really touching," I said. "I'll miss you, too. But I can't stay at school, and you can't come home with me. Here."

I pulled out a new drawing and taped it to the inside of my locker.

"If you get lonely, just look at this picture." It was me, but as a caveman, so it would fit in with the prehistoric

decor. (Look, of course *I* know that humans and dinosaurs lived millions of years apart, but Hamstersaurus Rex didn't!) He glanced at the Cave Sam I drew and then started gnawing my finger. For an ugly little mutant, he sure was cute.

"You're not making this any easier," I said.

"Who's not making what easier?" said Martha Cherie.

I slammed my locker shut. "Sorry," I said. "I was just, uh, talking on the phone."

"But you don't have a phone."

"I was practicing. For when I get one." I pantomimed answering. "Hello? No, this isn't Ethelbert Papageorgiou the Third. You must have the wrong number. Good-bye." I pretended to hang up. "How was that?"

"Good, but you probably should have asked what number they were trying to call," said Martha.

"Thanks," I said.

We stared at each other for a minute.

"Is there something I can help you with?" I said.

"When do you want to leave?"

"Leave?"

"For the Antique Doll Museum."

My heart sank. "That's today?"

Martha nodded.

"You know what, I'm actually feeling a little beat. Big week. Not sure if you remember, but I won Little Mister Muscles and singlehandedly defeated Beefer." I flexed. "Anyway, maybe we could reschedule. I'm thinking . . . June. Of next year."

Martha frowned. "The ADM is closed for the whole month of June for renovations. Besides, I already had my parents cancel conversational Portuguese and taxidermy and tap, just so we could do it today."

"Wow. You know how to tap-dance? I tried it once, and it's really hard," I said, feeling guilty.

Martha was right, I *had* promised.

"Actually, I'm getting a second wind," I said. "Let's meet at the museum at four."

"No need. We can ride over together," said Martha. "I brought my tandem bicycle."

"You brought it. To school," I said with a sigh. "The place where everyone I know is. That's— that's fantastic."

I grabbed my backpack, put my head down, and followed Martha. From the office I called my mom at work to tell her she wouldn't need to pick me up today. After a lot of questioning I grudgingly admitted I was going somewhere with an acquaintance who *happened* to be a girl. My mom giggled and told us to "have fun" in a weird voice, and my face got red. Seriously, calm down, Moms.

Thankfully, no one saw me and Martha ride off together down the street on her weird double bicycle. My newfound popularity was safe.

"I'm very close to finding Hamstersaurus Rex," said

Martha as we pedaled down the street.

"Did some new evidence come to light?"

"I analyzed Beefer's frayed sweatpants drawstring under my microscope. It was gnawed by the same second set of pointed teeth."

"But that's not Hamstersaurus Rex. It's some kind of freaky lizard, right?"

"Yes, but the tooth prints are too similar to discount. And I haven't seen any new hamster gnawings since early last week," said Martha. "I'm starting to think that the Hamstersaurus Rex we knew has *changed* somehow."

"Huh? No way," I said. "Here's what I think happened: somebody got a baby crocodile and tried to keep it as a pet, but it was too hard to take care of so they released it into the school sewer system and then it ate Hamstersaurus Rex and went to Florida so you don't need to worry about it anymore. The end."

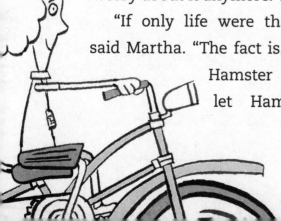

"If only life were that simple, Sam," said Martha. "The fact is, I failed at being Hamster Monitor when I let Hamstersaurus Rex escape. Now it's up to me to find him. If his teeth are pointy now, who knows what else might have changed. He could even be dangerous."

"He's not dangerous!" I said. "I mean, he's just a hamster, right?"

Martha nodded, but she didn't seem convinced.

We rode past the SmilesCorp international headquarters. It was an ultra-modern campus of buildings, all glass and brushed metal, on a hill overlooking town. I've been there a few times with my mom. The place always creeps me out.

Turns out the Maple Bluffs Antique Doll Museum was even creepier. It was housed in a run-down old mansion on an empty street near the edge of town. A faded banner out front displayed the museum's slogan: "Dolls Are Our Silent Friends!" Everything about the place made me feel like I was being watched. Once, I caught a faint whiff of something odd on the wind. Garlic? I glanced over my shoulder but there was nobody there.

"Great," said the ticket taker, sighing, as she saw us approach. "Martha Cherie: the reason we can *never* close early on Fridays."

"Good afternoon, Patricia," said Martha. "One child's ticket and one member." Martha held up her season pass. It was, of course, on a lanyard.

I unzipped my backpack to get my admission fee, and I was very surprised to see a little pair of eyes shining back at me.

"What are you *doing*?" I hissed at Hamstersaurus 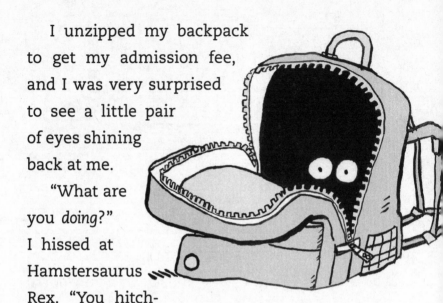 Rex. "You hitch-hiked? You should be at school!"

He made a little growl and waggled his stump arms and tried to look cute.

"No! Not cute! This is a disaster—"

"What's a disaster?" said Martha.

I quickly closed my backpack. "Nothing. I forgot, my, er, admission fee. Looks like I don't have five dollars, so I can't get into the museum. Sorry, I'll just catch the bus back—"

"Nonsense," said Martha. "I've prudently saved every dollar of birthday money I've ever received. I'm happy to cover you."

Martha pulled out a thick wad of bills and peeled off a five, which she placed on the counter. Patricia handed me a ticket.

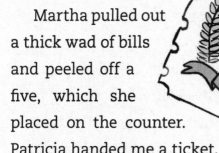

Inside, the ADM was even spookier. The twisting, dusty halls were deserted. It seemed like we were the only patrons. Maybe ever.

"This place is really informative, but it's a lot of fun, too," said Martha. "The exhibits start with the world's oldest dolls and each works its way forward in time. For example, this doll was made by the ancient Hittites." She pointed to a shriveled clay figurine behind a glass case.

"Cool," I said. "Do they have any, like, action figures here?"

159

Martha burst out laughing.

"Okay," I said. "Guess not."

We wound our way through corridor after corridor of musty old dolls. Many had patchy hair, missing limbs, and weird makeup on their faces. They ran the gamut from ominous to unsettling. Martha seemed happy, though.

"The best one is at the very end," said Martha. "An original 1958 Ginny Gossamer, informally known as history's most fragile doll. She's not behind any glass or anything. You feel like you could almost reach out and touch her, except that's totally against the rules."

On the second floor we passed a security guard, leaning against a wall.

"Good afternoon, Norton," said Martha.

"Argh!" cried Norton, apparently surprised to see another human being inside the Antique Doll Museum. "Oh, hi, Martha. Who's your little friend?" I noticed that he was holding an unopened bag of Flavor-Wedges.

"His name's Sam, and he's interested in becoming a doll collector," said Martha.

"It's not just a hobby but also an investment," said Norton to me.

"So I hear," I said.

Norton tore open his Flavor-Wedge bag, and I felt something stir. Not in my heart, but in my backpack. Hamstersaurus Rex sensed junk food nearby.

"You're going to love the Ginny Gossamer," said Norton, shoving a Wedge into his mouth and crunching down. "She's as delicate as a butterfly wing made of snowflakes—"

Against my will, I flew three feet toward him, backpack first. Norton blinked.

"Uh, hello again," I said.

"Hi," he said, taking an awkward step backward.

"Come on, Sam, next up is a really wonderful exhibit," said Martha. "It's called 'Dolls of the Eighteen Hundreds Whose Eyes Seem to Follow You.'"

I turned to go as Norton bit down on another Flavor-Wedge. Once again, Hamstersaurus Rex flung me toward him.

"Sorry," I said.

"Is something wrong, Sam?" asked Martha.

"Nope! Actually, come to think of it, I need to go to the bathroom," I said as I dashed off.

Of course, the bathroom was doll-themed (the paper towel dispenser was a giant porcelain clown face!). I unzipped my backpack. Hamstersaurus Rex looked half-crazy with hunger.

"Listen, dude," I said. "You've got to keep it together! You can't rampage. Not here. Not in front of Martha! Okay?"

Hamstersaurus Rex growled low and loudly. His pupils were fully dilated. His foot was twitching. What was it about junk food?

Just then, I heard movement behind me. I zipped up my backpack and turned around. Was someone else in the bathroom? I checked under the doors of all the stalls but saw no feet. The freaky towel dispenser face grinned at me from the corner. I shuddered and left.

I found Martha on the second-floor mezzanine, near the railing.

"Look at that," said Martha, admiring a grimy old doll with milky eyes under a glass case. She stepped from side to side. "They really do seem to follow you."

"Neat," I said. "But I should probably get going."

"Wait," said Martha, crossing her arms. "Sam, I think I know what's happening."

I paused. "You do?" I was ready to run.

"Absolutely," she said. "I saw how you kept lunging for Norton's food. I heard growling noises."

"You did?"

"Sure. You're famished. I'm a little hungry, too. Normally I choose healthy snacks like fresh beets or dried beets but there aren't any available, so I went to the first-floor vending machine and got us some snacks."

She reached into her purse and pulled out an array of prepackaged junk food.

"Wait!" I said. "No, that's not what I—"

But she'd already torn open a bag of Cheez Wallets. The salty artificial smell wafted toward me. I felt my backpack shudder.

"Stop!" cried a voice from the shadows.

Martha squinted toward the darkness. "You might be new here, but if this is about eating in the museum, I have *special permission*," she said, pulling out a handwritten letter from the board of trustees.

It was no doll museum security guard, however. Instead, Beefer Vanderkoff stepped out from behind a display case. He was wild-eyed and filthy, like he hadn't bathed the whole time he'd been absent from school. Weirdest of all, he had several strands of whole garlic cloves hanging around his neck. So someone *had* been following me after all.

"Oh," said Martha. "It's just you, Kiefer."

"Heed my words, Martha. You're not safe," said Beefer. "I just heard Sam talking to himself in the bathroom mirror. He was trying to convince himself not to 'rampage.' But then I heard him growl. Sam's a werewolf, and he wants to turn you into a werewolf just like him. Martha, he wants you to become his *eternal wolf bride!*"

"Werewolves aren't real," said Martha.

"Yes they are!" cried Beefer, putting himself between me and Martha. "It's all right here!" He held up the dog-eared "Werewolf Issue" of *Pustule* magazine.

My backpack was shaking wildly now, whipping back and forth on my shoulders. Hamstersaurus Rex was going crazy in there.

"It's cool, Martha," I said, backing away. "I'll just go."

"Sam, wait," she said. "You haven't even seen Ginny Gossamer yet!"

"Begone, foul beast-creature!" cried Beefer, waving a strand of garlic at me as he shoved Martha back.

"Garlic is for vampires," said Martha, "not werewolves."

"Really?" said Beefer, scratching his head.

"How can you not know that? Did you even read that magazine?" she asked.

"I skimmed it," admitted Beefer.

I started to run, but my backpack jerked me back toward them. Hamstersaurus Rex was losing control.

"Wait, Sam," said Martha. "At least eat your Cheez Wallets!" She shook the bag over her head, behind Beefer.

It was too much for Hamstersaurus Rex. He let out a thunderous dino roar.

"Oh no!" cried Beefer, pointing out the window. "The full moon rises! Sam is *changing!*"

The events of the next two seconds seemed to happen in slow motion. Hamstersaurus Rex burst through my backpack—he actually tore a hamster-shaped hole right through the canvas, like a cartoon—and I heard a high-pitched shriek. It wasn't Martha screaming, though. It was Beefer. A frenzied Hamstersaurus Rex hit the ground once and then leaped ten feet, right at the bag of Cheez Wallets in Martha's hand. A startled Beefer squealed, his garlic necklaces spinning around his neck. He stumbled backward and then disappeared over the mezzanine railing.

There was an instant of silence. Then I heard a crash below.

I ran to the edge of the railing. On the first floor Beefer lay on the ground on top of the remains of a splintered display stand. His eyes were wide open, staring up at nothing.

"Beefer, are you dead?" I cried.

He blinked and sat up. Not dead.

"Oh nooooooo," came Norton's pained wail, as he jogged toward Beefer on the floor below. "He landed on Ginny Gossamer. *He landed on Ginny Gossamer!*" Tears streamed from Norton's eyes as he stopped to pick up a single tiny doll arm. "She was too fragile for this world," he whispered with a sob.

"Got him!" cried Martha behind me.

I turned. Martha Cherie had taken a bulletproof glass case off the milky-eyed doll and capped it over Hamstersaurus Rex, who was still devouring the last of the Cheez Wallets.

As he licked his lips, Hamstersaurus Rex seemed to come to his senses. He looked around and realized that he was trapped. He charged at the glass. No effect. He roared, but the sound was weak and muffled. I saw panic in his little eyes.

"I can't believe it," said Martha, her eyes gleaming as eerily as any doll in the place. "I finally captured Hamstersaurus Rex!"

CHAPTER 15

IT WAS A gray Monday. I came to school with a sick feeling in the pit of my stomach. My locker dinosaur habitat was sadly empty; the stack of peanut butter and jelly sandwiches moldy and uneaten; the toy dinosaurs unchewed.

I made my way to homeroom without talking to anyone. When I got there, Martha Cherie stood at the front of the class grinning. Mr. Copeland was behind her, arms crossed. On the corner of his desk was a boxy shape covered by a drop cloth. Beefer glowered at me from the back row, one of his arms in a cast.

"Hello, children," said Mr. Copeland as we took

our seats. "Martha requested permission to hold a short press conference this morning before class. Obviously, I said 'No, that would be a terrible use of our time' and 'Sixth graders don't call press conferences.' But then her mother complained to the principal, so here we are. Martha, the floor is all yours."

"Thank you, Arnold," said Martha, reading prepared remarks from a set of note cards. "Good morning, classmates."

No one said anything.

"It is with great satisfaction that I report to you that our long, classroom-wide nightmare is over. On Friday night, at the Maple Bluffs Antique Doll Museum, I apprehended our escaped pet, Hamstersaurus Rex."

Martha whipped off the cloth, revealing a shiny new cage. Inside was Hamstersaurus Rex. His eyes darted around, stricken with fear. I felt like I might throw up my morning cinnamon toast. Martha waited, as though expecting applause. The room was silent.

I'd called her several times over the weekend,

trying to convince her that if she put Hamstersaurus Rex back in the classroom, he would fall prey to Beefer's revenge. Each time Martha assured me that he would be safe, and, more important, he would never escape again. Ever. She kept trying to change the subject to which antique doll was my favorite.

"Please, please. No need to thank me," Martha continued to read from her notes. "I was just doing my job, trying my best to live up to the sacred oath I swore on the day I became your class Hamster Monitor."

"Give me a break," muttered Dylan.

"Um, excuse me, but why was the hamster at some creepy museum, miles from the school?" asked Tina Gomez.

"That's an excellent question, Tina," said Martha. "Hamstersaurus Rex had—unbeknownst to Sam—hitched a ride inside of his backpack."

"Wait, you and Sam were at the museum . . . together?" said Omar.

"That's correct, Omar," said Martha. "We rode a tandem bicycle there. It was a date."

Everyone was looking at me now.

"Seriously?" said Dylan.

I shrugged and sank down in my seat. Somewhere behind me, I heard Beefer's teeth grinding.

"So what's going to stop Hamstersaurus Rex from escaping again?" asked Tina.

"Another excellent question," said Martha. "Mr. Copeland, may I give Tina a unicorn sticker?"

"Nope," said Mr. Copeland.

"The answer," said Martha, "is this." She waved toward Hamstersaurus's cage. "It's called the PETCATRAZ Pro™. I purchased it myself. Forged of unbreakable titanium, it's rated the world's strongest small-rodent cage. No hamster has ever escaped from a PETCATRAZ Pro™, that's the PETCATRAZ Promise. There are only two keys to this cage. As Hamster Monitor, I will keep one." Martha held up a key and then clipped it to the Hamster Monitor lanyard around her neck. "And Arnold will have the other."

She handed a second key to Mr. Copeland, who frowned and dropped it into his desk drawer.

"Are there any other questions?" asked Martha.

"Why does Hamstersaurus Rex look so gross now?" asked Caroline Moody.

"We're checking into that matter as part of an ongoing Hamster Monitor investigation," said Martha, scanning the room for more raised hands. "Jared?"

"Hypothetically, if someone *did* eat a pencil," said Jared Kopernik, "is it possible that person might gain magic pencil powers, such as the ability to erase time?"

"I'll handle this one, Martha," said Mr. Copeland, stepping forward. "No, Jared."

The day wore on. Martha allowed Hamstersaurus Rex only the food portion recommended by her uncle Tony, the hamster zoologist: half a lettuce leaf, twice daily. I knew that it wasn't nearly enough for Hammie Rex's mutant monster appetite.

Occasionally he threw a spectacular rampage inside of his cage, kicking up pine shavings and

pummeling his hamster wheel into an unrecognizable shape. But the PETCATRAZ Pro™ lived up to its promise. Even his incredible dino strength couldn't bend the bars.

After my tandem-bicycle, antique-doll "date" with Martha, I was once again relegated to the ranks of the uncool. I might be a loser, but at least I still had friends. Well, one friend. At lunch, I sat down beside Dylan.

"I have to think of a way to get Hamstersaurus Rex out of that cage," I said.

"Oh. And now you want me to help?" said Dylan.

"Well, yeah, I mean—"

"You're such a liar, Sam!" said Dylan. "You expect me to believe Hamstersaurus Rex was just hanging out in your backpack 'unbeknownst' to you?"

"Seriously, I had no idea," I said. I felt awful for deceiving my best friend yet again. "It's really weird, right?"

"You've been hiding Hamstersaurus Rex the whole time, haven't you? *That's* why you've been acting so weird these past weeks. Sneaking around. The extra food. You've been keeping him a secret from me."

"No way, I— Yeah. You're right." I sighed.

"Sam, we've been best friends for seven years," said Dylan. "Whenever you got made fun of, I stuck up for you. When everybody was so mad about those caricatures you drew, I defended you. Even when no one else would, I stood by you. But I guess you don't trust me. And now I can't trust you."

"No, we *can* trust each other," I said, struggling to explain. "It's just that after you accidentally revealed where Hamstersaurus Rex was hiding, well, I—I was worried you wouldn't be able to keep the secret."

"I made a mistake, and I said I was sorry, Sam. You should have given me a second chance."

"I know, but I was—I just . . ."

"Just *what?* Because as I understand it, *you're* the one who actually got Hamstersaurus Rex caught by Martha!"

That hurt a lot. Probably because it was true.

"Oh, and by the way, a tandem bicycle ride to the Antique Doll Museum with Martha Cherie?" said Dylan. "Gross!"

"I don't know. I promised." I shrugged and studied at the linoleum pattern of the cafeteria floor.

"And you promised me you were being honest!" She stood and picked up her lunch. "You know what the worst part is?"

"What?"

"I *could* have helped you with this whole thing. I could have helped protect Hamstersaurus Rex. I could have helped you deal with

Beefer. We could have thought all of this craziness through. Together. But you didn't let me." And with that, she left to find another table.

"Wait!" I said. But Dylan didn't look back.

It was the lowest I'd felt in quite a while. Don't worry, though, things were about to get even worse. Not thirty seconds after Dylan left, Beefer Vanderkoff sat down in her place.

"You must think you won, huh?" said Beefer.

"Nope," I said as I stared at my mashed potatoes. I guess he wasn't afraid of me anymore.

"Why? You got everyone to call me Urinal Head. You pretended like you were a werewolf just to make me look dumb. And then you stole my girl and practically broke my arm."

"That's not what happened!" I said, realizing that, wow, it sort of was.

"Well, laugh it up," said Beefer. "But you know what's going to be *really* funny? When I take that hamster out of its cage and flush it down the toilet today. That's right, it's Monday. Which means I've got after-school detention. All I need is one minute alone with that cage. Your precious

Hamstersaurus Rex is a goner, and you're not going to be there to stop it."

Beefer pounded the table once and left.

Back in class, Hamstersaurus Rex looked more pathetic than ever. I couldn't leave Beefer alone with him, not even for a moment. But how could I keep an eye on Hammie Rex during after-school detention? I'd be long gone by then.

Or would I? I sighed as I realized that I only had one option.

"Excuse me, Mr. Copeland," I said, raising my hand. "But I drew a picture of you."

"Uh, this is social studies class, but okay," said Mr. Copeland.

I held it up. I'd brought all my hard-won caricature skills to bear: it showed a crude image of Mr. Copeland with missing teeth, a ridiculous mustache, and a word balloon.

I never pay my parking tickets.

Mr. Copeland looked at the picture. "That's *extremely* hurtful, Sam. You know I can't grow a mustache."

"Also I just wanted to add that I, uh, think your tie is ugly," I said, trying for a surly, Beefer-ish tone.

"This tie was a gift from my late aunt," said Mr. Copeland, taken aback. "Purple-and-red parrots was her favorite color."

"Who cares," I said with a shrug. "School sucks!" Everyone in class stared at me now, utterly baffled.

"He's lost his mind," whispered Omar Powell.

"Mr. Copeland," said Martha, "even though

Sam and I are romantically linked, I just wanted to stress that his opinions are his own and they don't reflect my—"

"Hang on, Martha," said Mr. Copeland. "Sam, I'm confused. This really isn't like you."

"Yes it is. I'm not a quiet weirdo or even a popular cool guy anymore. I'm a misbehaving bad kid now. For example, check this out."

I jumped to my feet and grabbed Wally the class walrus puppet in one hand and a pair of safety scissors in the other. Then I tried my very best to snip off his left flipper. Of course, the safety scissors couldn't cut through the felt.

"Hang on," I said, struggling. "Almost got it. Just give me one more . . ."

"Put the walrus down, Sam," said Mr. Copeland.

"Fine," I said, dropping Wally. "But how about this?"

I grabbed a tube of glue off the shelf and twisted the cap so it was open. I waved it around menacingly. The other students leaned back in their desks.

"Easy, Sam," said Mr. Copeland.

When push comes to shove, I'm not a jerk. So I pointed the bottle back at myself and squirted it—all of it—right into my face. The whole class watched with a mixture of horror and disgust.

"Sam, you've left me no choice," said Mr. Copeland, "but to give you detention."

"Thanks," I said, taking my seat, feeling the glue drip down my neck.

Hamstersaurus Rex wouldn't be alone with Beefer after all.

CHAPTER 16

"NO TALKING.** NO laughing. No screaming. No singing. No whispering. No sleeping. No eating. No drinking. No chewing gum. No toys. No games. No puzzles. No word scrambles. No Sudoku. No electronic devices. No non-electronic devices. No cooking. No baking. No defrosting. . . ."

As Mr. Copeland read off the long list of rules of outlined in Horace Hotwater Middle School's Official After-School Detention Policy, I could feel a thin skin of dried glue still coating parts of my face. Despite what Jared Kopernik thought, I didn't enjoy the sensation of peeling it off.

It was my first detention. For the next two

hours, it would just be Mr. Copeland, Beefer Vanderkoff, and me: a standoff. I stared at Hamstersaurus Rex, crouched in his cage, looking hungry. He gave a low, pitiful growl. Could he feel the tension in the room? I snuck a glance at Beefer. He scowled at me so hard it looked like his face might break. Slowly, Beefer extended his index finger and pointed—despite the "no pointing" rule—at Hamstersaurus Rex. Then he drew the finger across his neck. I turned away.

"In the event that a student disobeys any of the stated detention rules, that student will earn two extra detentions, to be served at a later date. These future detentions are cumulative. If the student is unable to serve all detentions because he or she has graduated from Horace Hotwater Middle School, these detentions will transfer to whichever high school the student subsequently attends. In conclusion: discipline." Mr. Copeland took a deep breath. He had finally reached the end of the rules. "Beefer, obviously you've heard this many, *many* times before. Did you get all that, Sam?"

I opened my mouth to answer.

"No talking," said Mr. Copeland.

I closed my mouth and nodded to indicate that I understood.

"Fantastic," said Mr. Copeland. "If you need something from me, write it down on a piece of paper. Then raise your hand. I will come by and read your note." He smiled, cracked open a can of seltzer, and leaned back in his chair. "Hmm. Do you hear that?"

I shook my head.

"Exactly," said Mr. Copeland. "Utter silence. At home, my family talks over me. My next-door neighbors are always hammering things in the backyard. Here at school, I have to listen to you kids ask question after question, all day long, only occasionally interrupted by earsplitting bells. Detention is the only place where I get any peace and quiet. To tell you the truth, this is my favorite time of the week."

I nodded to indicate that I understood.

"And now, as always, I plan to read the newspaper," said Mr. Copeland as he unfolded it. "And drink a nice cold seltzer water." He took a sip and frowned. "Hmm. This seltzer seems to have gone flat. Both of you wait right here while I get another one from the soda machine. And in my absence, don't do any of the hundred and forty-six things I just mentioned."

He stood to leave. Beefer grinned; this would be his chance. I raised my hand and frantically scribbled something on a piece of paper. Mr. Copeland came to my desk to read my note. It said:

> Please let me buy you a seltzer. It's the least I could do after my shameful misbehavior earlier today. You should relax, Mr. Copeland. You work so very hard to educate us children.

He squinted at the note. "Ugh. This sounds like something your new girlfriend might write."

I opened my mouth to protest.

"No talking," said Mr. Copeland. "But okay. You

are hereby granted permission to buy me a can of seltzer." He handed me a dollar.

I walked extra slowly to the soda machine. I needed to run out the detention clock.

"This isn't seltzer," said Mr. Copeland, when I handed the can I'd bought to him. "It's grape soda."

I scribbled another note:

Sorry! The buttons are right next to each other and I have large thumbs. Let me rectify this terrible mistake by returning and buying you the correct beverage: Seltzer water.

"All right," said Mr. Copeland as he read it. "But hurry up." He handed me another dollar. Beefer looked like he wanted to kill me (even more than normal).

Once again, I made my way to the soda machine. This time I really did purchase a seltzer. But

I walked back so slowly I would have made Wilbur Weber's snails impatient. It took me ten minutes to travel the hundred yards back to the classroom.

"Sam, you took so long that I finished reading the newspaper!" said Mr. Copeland, annoyed. He tossed it into the recycling bin. "This detention is my 'me time.' Every Monday I enjoy a seltzer and read the paper, *simultaneously*. Now I have to go find something else to read while I drink this. Both of you wait here." He stood up to leave.

Again I raised my hand and frantically scribbled another note. It said:

Sorry again, Mr. Copeland! Please let me try to make this right by going to the school library and selecting something interesting to read while you enjoy your cold beverage. P.S. You've earned it! You're a great teacher and a very cool guy!

Mr. Copeland frowned as he read it. "Okay, fine," he said, plopping back down in his chair. "Go get me a book. Maybe a spy thriller. But, you know, funny."

Beefer was stewing as I left the classroom again. My plan was working. Maybe he wouldn't get his moment alone with Hamstersaurus Rex after all.

It took me a while to find an espionage comedy in the school library (*Day of the Cackle*; 1973).

"Thank you, Sam," said Mr. Copeland as I handed him the book. "I've heard very good things. It's supposed to be more exciting and even funnier than *The Thirty-Nine Yuks*."

I smiled and took my seat. Only forty-five minutes of detention left. It was starting to seem like Hamstersaurus Rex might survive the day. Hungry though he might be, the little guy looked calm and collected inside his cage.

Mr. Copeland stood up. "But now if you'll excuse me, I need to go to the restroom. I'll be back in a minute."

Again, I raised my hand and wrote a note. Mr. Copeland read it.

"Sam, I don't really understand how *you* going

to the bathroom for *me* would work." He crumpled it up and tossed it in the garbage.

Just then Beefer raised his hand. Mr. Copeland walked to his desk and read his note. He turned it sideways. Then upside down.

"Some of these aren't letters, Beefer. But if I understand your intention correctly, you want to go to the bathroom yourself?"

Beefer nodded.

"Fine," said Mr. Copeland.

Beefer stood to go. I hadn't considered that he might want to leave me and Mr. Copeland alone with Hamstersaurus Rex. What was he playing at? Beefer returned five minutes later and took his seat without a word.

It wasn't long after that when I smelled smoke.

"Is something burning?" cried Mr. Copeland, sniffing the air. "Hang on!" He leaped to his feet and dashed out the door.

In an instant, Beefer

was at the PETCATRAZ Pro™. Hamstersaurus Rex sensed the danger. His tail whipped, and he bared his fangs. Beefer grinned.

"I didn't think you had the guts to get a detention, Sam," said Beefer. "Too bad you still can't do anything to stop this. In fact, it's better this way. You'll get to watch." He grabbed the cage with his good hand and shook it. Inside, Hamstersaurus Rex snarled and puffed out his chest.

"Come on, Beefer," I said. "You don't need to hurt him."

"Together, you and this hamster ruined my life! People used to be afraid of me. Now they call me Urinal Head! They laugh when I walk by!"

"Hamstersaurus Rex was only trying to protect me," I said. "I'm the one you should be mad at. Not him!"

Beefer shook his head in disgust. "That might be the saddest part of all. You're nothing without this hamster, Sam. Just some weird loser with no friends who draws little pictures."

It stung. Maybe because he had a point.

"Now, just like *Wolfsplosion III*," said Beefer, turning

back to the cage, "this is going to end with violence."

"Beefer, please," I cried. "Don't do—"

I felt a flash of pain as Beefer socked me across the jaw. The next thing I knew, I was lying on the floor, dazed and blinking. Hamstersaurus Rex roared.

"Not so scary anymore," said Beefer. "Come on out, Martha Junior." He pulled on the locked cage door. It didn't budge. Beefer grunted and pulled harder. Nothing. He put the cage on the floor and put both his feet on it and pulled as hard as he could. The PETCATRAZ Pro™ held up. It was as good at keeping mutant hamsters in as it was keeping raging bullies out.

"You're not getting off that easy!" cried Beefer at last. He jammed his fingers through the tiny gaps in the bars. For a moment, Hamstersaurus Rex's eyes met mine. I swear the little guy winked at me— right before he chomped down on Beefer's index finger!

"Aaaaaaaaah!" Beefer squealed, ripping his hand back. The tip of his finger was bloody. "Hang on. I know how to get inside that cage!"

He threw open the drawer of Mr. Copeland's desk and began to rummage through his stuff. After a minute of this he stopped and grinned. The key caught the light as he held it up.

At that moment, we both heard a noise down the hall. Beefer swore, dropped the key, and slammed Mr. Copeland's drawer shut. Both of us scrambled back to our desks just in time.

"Beefer!" said Mr. Copeland, furious, his hands covered in soot, his purple-and-red-parrot tie singed at the end. "Did you start a fire in the water fountain?"

Beefer shook his head.

Mr. Copeland took a deep breath. "Look. I might not be able to prove that you did it. But I *know* it was you. So let this be your final warning: Beefer Vanderkoff, if you misbehave one more time—just one more time—you're suspended from school. Is that clear?"

Beefer nodded to indicate that he understood. Mr. Copeland noticed the cage key on his desk. He picked it up and put it into his bag.

Mr. Copeland didn't dare leave us alone again, even for a second. The rest of the detention passed smoothly. Hamstersaurus Rex glowered at Beefer from inside his cage, but Beefer didn't try anything else. Five minutes to go. I breathed a sigh of relief. The little guy would live another day.

But right before it was time to leave, I saw Beefer scribble a note. Instead of raising his hand, he simply left it on his desk. He'd written it for me.

I palmed the note as I walked past and only unfolded it once I was riding home in the car with my mom. It was only three words:

TUMOROW FINUL REVINGE.

CHAPTER 17

TUMOROW FINUL REVINGE.

The correctly spelled versions of those words ran through my head all night. I barely slept at all. What evil did Beefer have planned? The next morning I made my mom take me to school an hour early.

"Sam, I still don't understand why you squirted glue on your face," she said as she drove me. "Are you in a gang?"

"No, Mom."

"Is this about your little girlfriend?"

"Mom!"

"Okay, okay. I won't pry," she said. "But you

haven't been yourself lately. I'm worried about you, sweetie."

"You shouldn't be, Mom," I said, eager to get out as she pulled the car up to the school. "I've got everything under control."

"All right, I'll leave it alone," she said with a sigh. She handed me a ten-dollar bill from her purse. "This is for dinner—something healthy—since you won't be coming home before Science Night. I'll see you around five."

"Uh-huh. Wait, what? You're coming back?"

"Yes, honey. SmilesCorp asked for volunteers tonight. I'm so excited to see what your project is."

"Oh. Right. My project's awesome. Lots and lots of data. Maybe too much," I said, kissing her on the cheek. "Got to go." I hopped out of the car and ran toward the double doors of Horace Hotwater Middle School.

Beefer was neither early nor late. He arrived at school exactly on time. What diabolical master plan was he hatching?

I watched him closely all day long. The guy was on his absolute best behavior. That in and of itself was troubling. Once, he even raised his hand in class to answer a question. He got the answer wrong, of course—the capital of Pennsylvania isn't England—but it made my blood run cold all the same.

Dylan was right. I really could have used her help. I wanted to apologize. At lunch I tried to talk to her, but she turned her back and walked away before I could say a word. I ate cold tater tots alone.

Hammie Rex looked truly pathetic in his cage. When he growled it was more of a moan. Martha fed him his two half lettuces. Other than that he barely moved. The little guy seemed to be practically starving. I had to help him. But how?

"And I look forward to seeing what each of you has prepared for tonight," said Mr. Copeland, around an hour before school let out. "Word is that SmilesCorp is sending someone to demonstrate one of their new products for all of you. Should be quite the Science Night."

For some reason, those words snapped me out of my reverie. I raised my hand.

"Yes, Sam," said Mr. Copeland.

"Um, what exactly is Science Night?" I asked.

The whole class burst out laughing.

"Good one, Sam," said Mr. Copeland, chuckling. "See, you don't have to pour glue on yourself to get attention." And he continued our lesson about the French and Indian War.

Later, I found a poster on the bulletin board in the hall that answered my question. Beneath an image of a bubbling beaker, it read:

Horace Hotwater Sixth Grade Science Night

Tuesday, Nov. 3, 5 PM

A very large percentage of your science semester grade will be determined by the quality of your research! Don't miss this mandatory event! Presented by SMILESCORP®

"Corporations are people and people smile."

This was not good. Not good at all. With all the hamster drama, I had neglected to do anything for Science Night. Worse yet, my mom's job was sponsoring the event and she was volunteering. Today she would witness firsthand her only son flunking science in front of her professional colleagues.

So now I had three things on my plate. In order of importance: Preventing "FINUL REVINGE," saving Hammie Rex from starvation, and whipping up an impressive enough Science Night project before five o'clock to earn a passing grade. Yikes.

The bell rang, and Beefer left to go home. Just like that. No revenge. Not even an act of minor vandalism. Strange, but okay. Maybe he had a change of heart. Yeah, right. Anyway, I could check that one off the list for now.

Next I tried to sneak Hammie Rex a bag of Funchos Tangy Honey Habanero Flavor-Wedges. I never got the chance. Mr. Copeland met me at the door and shooed me away before I could get anywhere close to the PETCATRAZ Pro™.

"Sorry, Sam. I know detention was a barrel of laughs yesterday, but school's out and you can't be here right now. I'll see you at Science Night."

I left, but not before Hamstersaurus Rex caught a whiff of junk food. His pupils dilated. He foamed at the mouth and began to ricochet around his cage. I'd only made his hunger worse.

I was hungry myself—not hungry enough to rampage—but still pretty hungry. So I gobbled the Flavor-Wedges myself while I struggled to remember anything scientific I had learned in recent memory. Mutant hamster-dinosaurs came to mind.

Maybe I could whip up the gold standard of low-ambition science-fair projects: the old baking-soda-and-vinegar volcano. Except I didn't have any baking soda or vinegar. Or a volcano.

Could I grow crystals in water? No borax.

Electromagnetic nail? No battery.

Potato battery? No potato.

The clock was ticking. What *did* I have? I looked inside my locker. There I saw a bunch of toy dinosaurs, a stack of moldy five-day-old PB and Js, and ten pounds of sand.

Wait. Moldy sandwiches? What about the mold

guy, Alexander Fleming. Growing mold was science!

And so I set about creating the worst diorama of all time: the discovery of penicillin. At the center was a piece of white bread that had turned green and fuzzy. I wrote the word "Penicillin" underneath it. Beside that, the part of Alexander Fleming was played by a rubber triceratops. You couldn't tell who he was supposed to be so I wrote the words "Alexander Fleming" underneath him. The scene still didn't quite make sense, so I made a little cardboard top hat for the triceratops. I figured Alexander Fleming might have worn a top hat.

It was four forty-five by the time I finished writing the words "The Discovery of Penicillin" in glitter glue on the diorama. It looked pretty bad. I adjusted Alexander Fleming's hat.

In the gymnasium, there was a raised stage with a microphone and enough folding chairs for the whole grade. Principal Truitt and a couple of our teachers were already there. Other kids were already setting up their projects, many of which made mine look even worse. Omar Powell had made an electromagnetic nail. Caroline Moody had made a potato battery. I overheard Dylan explaining her project to Julie Bailey.

"I invented these ultra-lightweight prototype golf discs," said Dylan, holding one up. It was sleek and

red, beautiful. "According to my tests, they fly up to forty percent farther than anything available on the market. I feel like my discs could revolutionize the sport."

"It's not really a sport," said Julie.

"Yes it is!" I said before Dylan could. "By 2031, it will be more popular than devil sticks. Anyway, those discs look awesome, Dylan. Nice work."

"Thanks, Sam," said Dylan, before she remembered she was still mad at me. "I mean, whatever."

"Also, I wanted to tell you I'm really sorry for being a jerk," I said. "I shouldn't have lied to you. I hope you can forgive me."

Dylan stared at me and didn't say anything. Maybe she was still mad? At least I'd finally said what I needed to say. I sighed and walked on.

I saw Martha Cherie arranging seven poster boards outlining "Optimal Tuna Consumption for a Healthy Diet" with loads of charts and graphs and diagrams.

"There's room for you to set up your project

on the table next to mine, Sam," said Martha, absently twirling her Hamster Monitor lanyard with the cage key on it.

"You know what, I think I'll just put mine over there." I pointed to a spot between Wilbur Weber's project—a jar full of snails simply titled "SNAILS!"—and Jared Kopernik's, which seemed to be a three-foot ball of rubber bands with an ice-cream scoop sticking out of it (?). Yep, this was more the Discovery of Penicillin's league. It was the new pennies-and-plastic-wrap solar system.

With what I had—I'd at least put in the time required to grow mold, even if it was unintentional—I figured I could maybe pull a C-minus. Maybe. Embarrassing but not humiliating. I was starting to feel kind of okay about the whole thing.

Until I saw Beefer, that is. He was dragging a dirty wire cage across the floor of the gym. The cage appeared to be full of heavy, gray rope. No, not rope. Rope doesn't move. I caught the flash of a yellow eye.

He'd used Science Night as a pretext to bring his pet boa constrictor to school. Now I knew exactly what "FINUL REVINGE" he had in mind: Beefer Vanderkoff meant to feed Hamstersaurus Rex to his giant snake.

CHAPTER 18

MY HEART WAS pounding. I had to stop Beefer. I couldn't let Hamstersaurus Rex end up as dinner for a boa constrictor. I didn't know how, but I had to think of a way to—

"There he is!" cried Coach Weekes, startling me. "Little Mister or Miss Muscles himself!"

I turned. Weekes was standing next to my mom and a slick-looking woman in a shiny business suit. She was holding a metal briefcase and fiddling with her smartphone. Behind them stood a professional photographer in cargo shorts.

"Hi, Sam," said my mom, waving. "What's all this I'm hearing about your little muscles?"

"Nothing, Mom," I said, trying to keep an eye on Beefer across the gym.

"Muscly and modest, too!" said Coach Weekes, slapping me on the back. "Sam here did the Sixty-Foot Sand Bag Drag in seven-point-seven seconds. *Seven-point-seven!* Can you believe it?"

"I can't. My son didn't mention dragging anything," said my mom. "Finally, some good news from school. So Sam *won* something?"

"Not just *something*, Ms. Gibbs," said Coach Weekes. "He won Little Mister or Miss Muscles, the preeminent junior fitness competition of the twentieth century."

"But . . . it's the twenty-first century," said my mom, confused.

The slick-looking woman suddenly stopped messing with her phone and seemed to notice me. "Hi, Sam, extremely pumped to meet you. My name is Roberta Fast," she said, shaking my hand a little too hard. "I'm a marketing rep, and I work with your mom at SmilesCorp. I'll be the one presenting you with your award tonight."

"Award?" I said.

"Your Little Mister or Miss Muscles Trophy," said Coach Weekes, squinting at me. "The fine people of SmilesCorp ponied up the thirty-five dollars to have it made. You *did* remember that this was happening tonight, didn't you, Sam?"

"Oh yeah, absolutely," I lied. "Of course."

"So, first I'm going to give your class an exclusive first look at a top secret new SmilesCorp product that I'm both psyched and jazzed to promote," said Roberta. "After that, I'll introduce you. You can make a few prepared remarks. Then I'll hand over the trophy and Topher here can snap a few pictures for our social media accounts." She pointed to the photographer.

"Maybe he could get a photo of my calf muscles, too," said Coach Weekes, turning around and flexing them.

Roberta stared at him blankly. "Wait. Who are you, again?"

"I'm Coach Weekes," said Coach Weekes, frowning.

"Hang on," I said. "I think I missed something. Did you say *prepared remarks?*"

"Sure, just give a short acceptance speech," said Roberta. "No more than three, maybe four minutes. Try to keep it light, funny. But heartfelt and touching too."

"Three or four minutes . . . of me talking," I said. Now my Hamstersaurus anxiety was spiked with a good-sized dose of stage fright.

"You *did* prepare some remarks to remark," said Coach Weekes, squinting again.

"Uh-huh," I said.

"My son, delivering an acceptance speech!" said my mom as she gave me a big hug.

"That's fantastic," said Roberta. "Mother and son: a SmilesCorp family. Topher, get a shot of that. We can run it with a caption like 'Mama Muscles.'"

Topher snapped a picture. Roberta checked her phone.

Principal Truitt approached us. She can be scary, but she has a healthy

disdain for Beefer Vanderkoff. I respect that.

"Good evening, Ms. Gibbs, Ms. Fast," said Principal Truitt. "Whenever you're ready, we can begin the presentation."

"Fantastic," said Roberta Fast. "Showtime."

Before I realized what was happening I'd been ushered onto the stage by Coach Weekes. My mom gave me a thumbs-up and took a seat beside Mr. Copeland and the other kids in the folding chairs.

"Everyone, I'd like you to all give a very warm welcome to Roberta Fast from SmilesCorp," said Principal Truitt.

"Good evening!" said Roberta as she took the mic. "I'm totally psyched to be here at Horace Hotwater Middle School, the greatest middle school in the history of humanity!"

This got a big round of applause. I tried to keep Beefer in my sights while simultaneously thinking of a light, funny, heartfelt, touching, three-to-four-minute speech.

"I'd sure rather be at Horace Hotwater than at"— Roberta glanced down at her smartphone—"L. L.

Dupree Middle School, down the road. Boooooo!"

The crowd booed along with her. Roberta Fast had read the room correctly. We Horace Hotwater students are supposed to despise L. L. Dupree, three miles away. They are our hated rivals for some reason that has never been fully explained.

"So, who here is a fan of the SmilesCorp family of food and beverage products?" asked Roberta.

The crowd gave a tepid response.

"I'll ask that question a different way. Who here enjoys *Funchos Flavor-Wedges*? How about *Choconobs*? Or *Cheez Wallets*?"

The crowd exploded. Kids love junk food. Hamstersaurus Rex might have applauded, too, if he'd been around. And his arms weren't so stumpy.

"All of those beloved snacks were created in SmilesCorp labs," said Roberta. "Er, I mean test kitchens—obviously kitchens. Because it's food!"

The crowd murmured at her slip up. Roberta continued as though nothing had happened. "And even though SmilesCorp is an international corporation operating in over a hundred and fifty countries worldwide, we are headquartered right here in Maple Bluffs, the greatest town in the history of humanity!"

The crowd went nuts again. She'd won them back.

"Now, I'm about to give you an exclusive first look at the newest, most radical snack food item that will have huge appeal among your demographic. No one outside SmilesCorp has ever seen what I'm about to show you, and we think you kids can create some advance buzz on social media. Are you pumped?"

Everyone cheered to indicate pumpedness. Not me, though. I felt a growing sense of panic. Out in the audience Beefer was shifting in his seat. He looked like he was ready to make his move.

"Without further ado," said Roberta Fast, "I present to you: a prototype food so revolutionary that we at SmilesCorp believe it will *change the way the world snacks forever!*"

She nodded off to the side. From somewhere, dramatic music began to play. Roberta deliberately placed her metal briefcase on the podium.

"Behold," she said as she threw open the lid, "the *invisible doughnut!*"

The briefcase was empty. The crowd was silent.

"Let's hear it for the invisible doughnut!" said Roberta.

"We can't see anything," said Tina Gomez.

"Exactly," said Roberta. "That's what makes this snack so incredible. It is completely invisible to the naked eye." She reached into the briefcase and pinched her thumb and forefinger together, then she made the motion of lifting something.

At this, the crowd went "Ooooooh." Topher snapped a photo.

"How does it work?" asked Jimmy Choi.

"Awesome question. Pumped you asked," said Roberta. "Obviously we start with the finest-quality doughnuts. Then we give them a special coating of color-changing *chromatophores* derived from *Bothus lunatus*. That way, the doughnut can exactly match the pattern of its surroundings, effectively rendering it invisible."

She turned the doughnut this way and that and gave a bright smile. This drew massive applause.

Martha Cherie raised her hand.

"Yes, you there, little girl," said Roberta to Martha. "Question?"

"Hi. Martha Cherie, honor student," said Martha. "I might be mistaken, but isn't *Bothus lunatus* the scientific name for a species of Atlantic flounder that camouflages itself to avoid predators?"

Roberta was taken aback. "Okay, I can't confirm or deny that, but I promise you I will check on our end to see if what you're saying is, uh, accurate. Anyway, the invisible doughnut's special coating doesn't just come from *Bothus lunatus*. I'm told it also uses some chromatophores from *Sepia apama*."

Martha raised her hand again.

"Anybody else have a question?" said Roberta, looking around.

Nobody did.

"Yes, fine," said Roberta. "You again."

"Isn't *Sepia apama* actually just the scientific name for the giant cuttlefish, which is pretty much like a squid?" said Martha. "Did SmilesCorp make the doughnut invisible by using genetically engineered fish and cephalopod DNA? Because, honestly, that seems kind of gross to me."

"Fish doughnut," said Wilbur Weber. "Blech!"

Someone laughed.

"It doesn't affect the taste!" said Roberta Fast. And just like that, she'd lost them. Nobody was listening now. They were all making wisecracks and pretending to throw up. Mr. Copeland was struggling to calm them.

"Everyone, settle down!" commanded Principal Truitt.

"Okay," said Roberta. "You know what, no further questions. We have, uh, let's go ahead with—"

"Is the doughnut alive?" asked Martha.

"No further questions!" said Roberta.

Topher snapped a picture. Roberta shrieked.

"What happened?" asked Principal Truitt.

"I dropped it!" cried Roberta, scanning the ground. "I dropped the invisible doughnut. Nobody move!"

"Is it on the stage?" asked Coach Weekes, looking at the ground himself.

"I don't know! It's invisible!" said Roberta. "It could have rolled somewhere."

"Nobody move," said Principal Truitt.

"This is bad," said Roberta. "This is really bad. That doughnut was a prototype. If I don't get it back to the lab I'm going to be in trouble."

"Should I call a manager?" asked my mom.

"Absolutely not!" said Roberta. "We have to find it!"

"Everyone stand up," said Principal Truitt. "I need you to all look underneath your seats."

And so everyone at Science Night spent ten minutes looking for a doughnut that can "exactly match the pattern of its surroundings." Nobody found the thing. Honestly, I was starting to doubt that invisibility was such a good idea for a new snack.

Roberta stood on the stage, texting frantically. "This is bad. This is really bad. This is really, *really* bad," she muttered to herself.

I couldn't have agreed more. By now, Beefer had crept up behind Mr. Copeland, who was still searching for the invisible doughnut. He was going to try to steal the PETCATRAZ Pro™ cage key! I started to leave the stage.

"Hold on," said Coach Weekes, stopping me.

"Where are you going, Gibbs?"

"I feel sick," I said.

"That's just nerves," said Coach Weekes. "If you hope to make a career as a professional body-builder, you're going to need confidence."

"Okay . . . What if I *don't* hope to do that?"

Coach Weekes laughed. "Good one! Now get out there, Gibbs, and seize the title you were born to hold: Little. Mister. Or. Miss. Muscles."

He shoved me toward the mic.

Without looking up from her phone, Roberta mumbled, "SmilesCorp proudly presents the award to this kid."

She tossed me the trophy—a heavy slab of marble shaped like the SmilesCorp smile. On the plaque they had misspelled my name: "Sar Gibbs."

"Uh," I said.

The microphone squealed. I blinked. Everyone in the audience stopped looking under their seats and stared at me. Behind Mr. Copeland, Beefer was now rummaging around in his bag for the key.

"I'll keep it short," I said. "Thanks!"

I held up the trophy then I turned to go. Behind

me I saw Coach Weekes glaring. He tapped his watch. I stopped.

Out in the audience, something glinted between Beefer's sausage-like fingers: he'd found the PETCATRAZ Pro™ key. I had to do something, *anything*!

"I may have won this award," I said, turning back toward the audience and talking at double speed, "but I couldn't have done it without the help and guidance of a very special mentor of mine. A hero, really, who inspired me every step of the way . . ."

"Gibbs, you're too kind," said Coach Weekes, stepping forward.

"Of course I'm speaking," I said, "of Kiefer 'Beefer' Vanderkoff."

The whole crowd turned to look at Beefer now. Startled, he palmed the key.

"What?" cried Coach Weekes.

"Wait. Doesn't Beefer hate you?" asked Wilbur Weber, confused.

"You're so dead, Sam," said Beefer.

"Excuse me, Mr. Vanderkoff?" said Principal Truitt.

"It's nothing. Beefer is just razzing me," I said. "Right, old buddy?"

"Yep," said Beefer, gritting his teeth.

"For all his help and support," I said, "I honestly think this trophy belongs more to him than it does to me. Why don't you come up here and accept the award, Beefer?"

"No, thanks," said Beefer.

"Get up there, Mr. Vanderkoff," said Principal Truitt. "Now."

Reluctantly, Beefer mounted the stage, the key still clutched in his fist. We stared at each other in silence. My heart raced. I knew I was going to earn a pounding for this.

"Congratulations," I said as I handed Beefer the Little Mister or Miss Muscles trophy. At the same time, I lunged forward and attempted to pry the key out of

his clenched fist. We struggled awkwardly for a moment.

"I guess they're . . . hugging?" said Julie Bailey, sounding baffled.

I managed to get two fingers on the key, but Beefer was just too strong for me (not to mention how sweaty his palms were . . . yuck). He yanked his fist away, and I stumbled backward, empty-handed.

"Ha! I've still got the—" said Beefer, panting. He suddenly remembered the whole school was watching. "The trophy. I've got the trophy. Thanks to my good buddy, Sam Gibbs."

He grinned at me and slid the hidden key into his pocket.

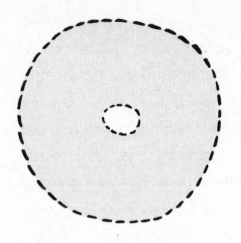

CHAPTER 19

BEEFER STOOD ON the stage, awkwardly posing with the LMMM trophy while Topher snapped photos.

"Um, maybe you could, you know, *smile* for this next one?" said Topher. "After all, we are called *SmilesCorp.*"

Beefer did something with his mouth that wasn't a smile—come to think of it, the guy didn't smile much outside the con-text of evil schemes. Topher sighed.

Mr. Copeland and the other sixth-grade teacher, Ms. Maddox, were now grading students' experiments. Their "guest judge," Roberta Fast, didn't seem to be helping much as they tested Omar's electromagnetic nail. Instead, she muttered and texted and continued to search in vain for the invisible doughnut. My mom sat at a table passing out SmilesCorp brochures to students and looking worried.

Beefer's photo session wouldn't last much longer. I needed to free Hamstersaurus Rex before he could. Unfortunately, that meant I had to get the other key.

"Hiya, Martha," I said, sidling up to her exhibit.

"Hello, Sam," she said. As always, her Hamster Monitor lanyard hung around her neck. The second PETCATRAZ Pro™ key dangled from it.

"Your exhibit is very cool. I had no idea that tuna was a great source of selenium *and* niacin."

"Thanks! Your exhibit is, um . . ." She trailed off. "Anyway, that was very magnanimous of you to dedicate your trophy to Kiefer, even though he thinks you're a werewolf. And in case you don't know what 'magnanimous' means—since your vocabulary is probably smaller than mine—it's the same as generous."

"Thanks. Say, there was something you said to me once that I've been thinking a lot about recently. You said that one day I might be able to make Junior Deputy Hamster Monitor."

"Sure. With hard work and dedication, anything is possible."

"If that happened," I said, "would I get my own ID lanyard?"

Martha's eyes lit up. "Of course you would, Sam."

"I know it's a little weird, but . . . could I try on your Hamster Monitor lanyard, just to see how it feels?"

She was taken aback. "I don't know, Sam," said Martha. "That would be highly unorthodox."

Onstage, Beefer was reluctantly pantomiming the various Little Mister or Miss Muscles feats for the camera. He'd already gotten to the Sandbag Drag. I only had a few seconds left.

"Please," I said to Martha. "Please, please,

please, please can I try on the lanyard?"

Martha looked around to make sure nobody was watching. She took a deep breath. Very quickly she slipped off her lanyard and put it around my neck.

"Wow, I can feel the weight of responsibility on my shoulders," I said. "I realize now that Hamster Monitor is a sacred trust."

"Exactly!" said Martha.

"Okay, cool, here you go, bye!" I said, tossing the lanyard back to her. Luckily she didn't notice that it was lighter—by the weight of one key.

A moment later, I was racing down the hallway toward Mr. Copeland's classroom. Thankfully, the lock on the door was still broken.

Inside, I saw Hamstersaurus Rex. He sat up in his cage and roared.

"Good to see you, too, pal," I said as I turned the key and opened the PETCATRAZ Pro™. Hamstersaurus Rex sprang into the air, turned a flip, and landed on the ground.

"Go, my prehistoric friend!" I said as I followed Hamstersaurus Rex out into the hall. "You're free!"

"Free lunch," said Beefer. He stood in Hamster-saurus Rex's path with his boa constrictor coiled around his neck. "Guess I didn't need this after all." Beefer stuffed Mr. Copeland's key back into his pocket. "Thanks for unlocking the cage for me, Sam."

"Run, Hammie Rex!" I cried.

"Not so fast. I want to introduce you to a friend of mine," said Beefer. He tossed his boa constric-tor onto the floor. The snake was huge—probably eight feet long—with gray and red scales. It slith-ered toward Hamstersaurus Rex, whose fur stood on end. "Meet Michael Perkins!" said Beefer.

"Hang on," I said. "Your pet snake's name is Michael Perkins?"

"Yeah. So what? What's wrong with that?"

"I don't know. Just kind of a weird thing to call a snake."

"Well, Hamstersaurus Rex is a weird thing to call a hamster!"

"True," I admitted.

"Anyway, shut up!" cried Beefer. "Hamstersau-rus Rex might be strong now, but Michael Perkins is even stronger. In the wild, boa constrictors eat, like, elephants and junk! Once my snake gets ahold of your hamster, he'll crush him and swallow him. Then I'm going to make you watch while Michael Perkins slowly digests Hamstersaurus Rex for the next four to six hours!"

Beefer caught me by the shirt and slammed me against a row of lockers. Hamstersaurus Rex snarled at him and bared his fangs. Michael Perkins coiled to strike.

"Don't worry about me, Hamstersaurus Rex," I said. "Just go!"

Hamstersaurus Rex gave a growl. Michael Perkins struck, and Hammie Rex barely managed to scramble out of the way.

"Go on!" I cried again. "Go!"

Hamstersaurus Rex dashed off down the hallway with the boa constrictor slithering close behind. I wriggled out of Beefer's grasp and ran after them. They'd already rounded the corner and raced down the stairs. I got to the first floor just in time to see them dash through the open door of the gymnasium.

"Oh no," I said to myself. They'd blundered right into Science Night!

Hamstersaurus Rex skidded to a halt under the table holding Jimmy Choi's borax crystal project. No one had seen him.

Plenty of people noticed Michael Perkins, though. He elicited screams from frightened children as he snaked across the gym floor, tongue flicking. I reached down to grab the boa with two hands and tried to hold him back. With a hiss and a quick flick of his body, Michael Perkins easily threw me off. The boa probably weighed as much as I did, and Beefer wasn't lying: he was at least as strong as Hammie Rex.

"Snake!" screamed Omar Powell. "Snake, snake, snake!"

"What's going on?" said Principal Truitt. But Michael Perkins had disappeared under another table. I made a break for Hamstersaurus Rex.

"The exit's that way," I hissed at him as I pointed frantically back the way he had come.

"Yeah, I can read the sign, Sam," said Jimmy Choi, shaking his head.

Hamstersaurus Rex seemed to understand me, though. He started to turn, but then he caught a whiff of something on the air. His nose twitched. His little pupils dilated. A strand of drool formed at the corner of his lips. I knew that look. He smelled junk food. This wasn't good. Not good at all. Instead of leaving, Hammie Rex charged toward the stage and leaped up onto the podium.

"Hey! It's Hamstersaurus Rex!" cried Dylan.

"What?" cried Martha. "But no hamster has *ever* escaped from a PETCATRAZ Pro™. The PET-CATRAZ Promise has been broken!"

Hamstersaurus Rex opened his jaws wide and bit down on nothing at all. Then he started to chew.

"Aaaaagh!" shrieked Roberta Fast. "That renegade hamster is eating my invisible doughnut! *It is eating my invisible doughnut!*"

I guess Ham-
mie Rex's highly
attuned sense of smell
could detect refined
carbohydrates and arti-
ficial colors even if they
couldn't be seen. Now
he was gobbling down the
snack food of the future.

"Fish doughnut," said Wilbur Weber. "Blech."

At that moment, the boa constrictor slowly rose
up behind Hamstersaurus Rex, fangs glistening.

"Look out, Hammie Rex!" I screamed. "It's Michael Perkins!"

"Who?" said Julie Bailey.

Hamstersaurus Rex turned just in time and
leaped out of the way. Michael Perkins struck at
exactly the spot where he had been standing. The
snake swallowed an invisible lump: the other half
of the SmilesCorp doughnut.

Everyone in the gymnasium stared at the
two creatures for a moment. Then both of them
disappeared.

CHAPTER 20

THE GYM FELL SILENT. We'd just seen two living creatures turn invisible before our very eyes.

"Whoaaaaaaa," said Drew McCoy.

"Um. Is that what the doughnut is supposed to do?" asked Mr. Copeland.

"It's just a prototype. We're still in testing," said Roberta Fast. "No more questions!"

At that moment, the deafening sound of my mother's first sneeze rang out across the gym.

"Was that a gun?" cried Coach Weekes as he hit the floor, covering his head.

"Sorry," I said. "My mom's allergic to hamsters!"

Just then, a hole burst right through the middle of Omar Powell's electro-magnetic nail display. I heard a dino roar. It was Hammie Rex and Michael Perkins—even though they were invisible, the chase was still on!

"Eek!" squealed Coach Weekes, now leaping into the air. "Something invisible touched my calf muscles!"

Tina Gomez's homemade barometer was smashed to pieces right before her very eyes. My mother sneezed again. From somewhere Hamstersaurus Rex gave another roar. I ran toward the sound.

An invisible commotion tore through Science Night, flattening projects and shredding hand-lettered poster boards.

Caroline Moody saw that her potato battery was right in the path of the two creatures, so she yanked it out of the way. Unfortunately, as she did, she tripped over the wires and fell right on top of it. It was a mashed potato battery now.

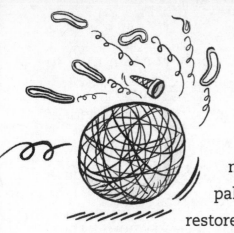

The swath of destruction rolled on. Children screamed. Beakers shattered. Tables flipped. My mother sneezed. Principal Truitt tried in vain to restore order.

"Everyone, remain calm!" she bellowed. "It's just two invisible animals locked in a fight to the death. There is no reason to get excited, people!"

I followed behind Hammie Rex and Michael Perkins, hoping that I could do something, anything, to save the little guy from being eaten alive. Martha Cherie was right behind me.

"Stop, in the name of the law!" she yelled at the hamster and the boa constrictor as she waved her Hamster Monitor ID. They ignored her authority.

Roberta Fast was behind her, eyes wild. "We need to catch both of those creatures and pump their stomachs!" she said. "They have eaten SmilesCorp intellectual property!"

Three more Science Night projects went down, including Martha's—now the students of Horace

Hotwater would never know how much tuna to eat. "The Discovery of Penicillin" was next, instantly crushed flat by the invisible commotion. Eleven minutes of hard work gone in a single instant. Wilbur Weber's jar exploded, scattering snails across the floor of the gym.

"Snaaaaaaaails," he wailed. His plaintive cry was drowned out by the nonstop sound of my mom sneezing.

I heard another roar, then an abruptly strangled squeak. Followed by nothing.

"Hammie Rex!" I cried. "Are you okay?"

Near Jared Kopernik's giant rubber band ball, a gray shape began to shimmer and materialize.

"Look! The effects of the invisible doughnut

are wearing off," cried Dylan.

The gray shape became clearer. I could see that it was Michael Perkins. Inside his belly there were now two lumps.

One was half-doughnut sized. The other was the size of a hamster.

CHAPTER 21

MICHAEL PERKINS SAT on top of the rubber band ball, tongue flicking. The gym fell silent. Even my mom stopped sneezing.

"No," I whispered.

I felt despair creeping into my guts. I couldn't believe it. It wasn't happening. It wasn't fair! We were supposed to be friends forever. And yet, there was no denying the hamster-shaped lump in the boa's stomach.

Beside me, Martha gasped and dropped her lanyard. The other kids in my class looked dumbstruck. I blinked back tears. I'd promised I would look out for Hamstersaurus Rex, that I wouldn't let anyone hurt him. But I hadn't kept that promise. I'd failed him.

"Sam, I'm so sorry," said Dylan, putting her hand on my shoulder.

I didn't know what to say. I was crying now, and I didn't try to hide it. Hamstersaurus Rex was gone. He was gone.

There on the ground nearby was my crushed diorama. The moldy peanut butter and jelly sandwich was smeared across rumpled cardboard. I blinked. Something from "The Discovery of Penicillin" was missing . . .

At that moment, Michael Perkins gave a weird hiccup and a strangled burp. Then he shuddered and barfed out a slimy rubber triceratops complete with cardboard top hat. The second lump in his stomach was Alexander Fleming! In the ruckus he must have eaten the toy dinosaur. Then that meant—

"There he is!" cried Tina Gomez.

With a shimmer of orange, Hamstersaurus

Rex reappeared on the stage. He let out a triumphant roar. The whole class broke out in applause.

But the battle wasn't over. In an instant, Michael Perkins was on him again. The snake circled around Hamstersaurus Rex, rising up to strike. Hamstersaurus Rex didn't run this time. He snarled and snapped at Michael Perkins, who slithered backward, waiting to make his move.

Then, in one lightning-quick motion, Michael Perkins somehow coiled himself around Hamstersaurus Rex's body. Hammie Rex shook and squirmed and gave another growl, but it was weaker this time. Michael Perkins tightened his hold. Now the little guy couldn't make a sound. He struggled, but he couldn't get free.

"He's being crushed!" I cried.

Michael Perkins opened his jaws wide—wider than seemed possible—and shifted Hamstersaurus

Rex toward his mouth. I started to run toward the stage, but I realized I would never make it in time.

I had to think of something quick. I looked back over my shoulder as I ran and saw Dylan, clutching her homemade golf disc to her chest.

"Dylan!" I cried. "Throw it!"

She knew exactly what I meant. Dylan took a deep breath and squinted toward the stage for a second. Then she let it fly. All eyes in the gym followed the disc as it cut a perfect line—a hundred feet, straight through the air—and lodged in Michael Perkins's open mouth!

Michael Perkins couldn't close his jaws. He flopped around the stage, failing to dislodge the disc that stretched his mouth open. Hamstersaurus Rex wriggled out of his coils.

"Wow, D'Amato!" said Coach Weekes. "What a throw!"

"See, Coach, it is a sport!" said Dylan.

Without the use of his fangs, Michael Perkins was helpless. He started to slither away, but Hamstersaurus Rex stomped on the tip of his tail, stopping him dead. With a roar of Jurassic rage, Hamstersaurus Rex chomped down hard on Michael Perkins's tail. Then he started to spin, faster and faster. Soon Michael Perkins was whipping around him like a rubbery propeller. At last, Hamstersaurus Rex released his bite. The boa constrictor sailed right out the open window of the gymnasium.

Science Night exploded! Hamstersaurus Rex stomped around in little circles, soaking up the attention. He waved his stumpy arms and whipped his tail.

"Yes!" I yelled.

A chant broke out among the sixth graders of Horace Hotwater: "Hamstersaurus Rex! Hamstersaurus Rex! Hamstersaurus Rex!"

"We have to find that snake!" shrieked Roberta

Fast as she rushed out toward the parking lot, dragging my poor sneezing mom and Topher—snapping pictures as he went—with her.

I picked up Hamstersaurus, midstrut.

"I'm glad you're okay, little buddy," I said. "I really missed you."

"Mrrrrgghhhnnng," he replied, which probably meant something very touching in mutant Hamsterese. He leaped into the air, turned a flip, and landed in my pocket. I rubbed his belly and scratched behind his ear at the same time.

Meanwhile, the other kids were cheering and laughing and hugging one another. Mr. Copeland was doing a silly dance with Ms. Becker. Coach Weekes was flexing his calf muscles in time. Even Principal Truitt was giggling in a very un-principal-like manner. Suddenly, her nose twitched.

"Hang on," she said. "Is that smoke?"

I sniffed the air. She was right. Something somewhere was burning.

"I know that smell," said Principal Truitt, slowly resting her face in her palm.

"Water fountain fire," said Mr. Copeland and

Coach Weekes in unison.

"Beeeeeeefer!" bellowed Principal Truitt at the top of her lungs. Then she dashed out into the hallway. Mr. Copeland, Ms. Maddox, and Coach Weekes raced after her, leaving the gym adultless.

The door of the gymnasium swung closed after them. Of course, Beefer Vanderkoff stood behind it. The crowd fell silent.

"Sam," said Beefer, pointing at me with the SmilesCorp trophy. "It's time we settled this once and for all."

"Yeah," I said. "I guess it is."

"Whatever, Beefer," said Dylan. "Sam kicked your butt before, he can do it again!"

"Ha," said Beefer. "He only beat me because of that dumb gerbil!"

A murmur ran through the crowd.

"Yeah," I said. "That's true."

"And I'd bet my *Wolfsplosion II* DVD that he didn't really win that Muscles thingy, either! That was the gerbil, too, wasn't it, Sam?"

I sighed. "Yep. It was."

"See, everyone? He's nothing. Pathetic. A total fraud," said Beefer. "Just a weird loser with no friends who draws little pictures."

The gym was quiet. The other kids stared at me now.

"Sam has friends," said Dylan, stepping forward.

"Yeah," said Martha. "He does."

Beefer winced at this.

"You humiliated me, Sam," said Beefer. "Now it's your turn. The *final*, final revenge. I'm going to pound you—in front of your precious gerbil and the whole school—and there's not a thing you can do about it."

Hamstersaurus Rex snarled, ready to defend me. I put my hand on his head to calm him.

"You're right, Beefer," I said. "I'm not very tough. You can definitely beat me up."

Beefer gave a joyless yellow grin. He cocked back his fist to scare me. I didn't flinch.

"But even so," I said, "I've decided I'm not going to be afraid of you anymore."

"What?" said Beefer. "But you can't just *decide* to—"

"Beefer, the weird thing is," I said, "we're actually kind of alike."

"You take that back!" said Beefer, horrified.

"We are," I said. "Think about it. We're both into stuff that other people don't get. In my case it's mutant hamsters and drawing 'little pictures'; in yours it's exploding werewolves and vandalism."

"Those things couldn't be more diff—"

"We don't quite fit in. We want people to like us, and it hurts our feelings when they don't."

"What? No way!" said Beefer, his voice high and frantic. "I don't have feelings!"

"But hurt feelings is no reason for me to pretend like I'm something I'm not," I said. "And it's no reason for you to act like a jerk."

The other kids were starting to whisper. I could see the color drain from Beefer's face. His whole world was slipping away, and he didn't know what to say.

"I am a clear belt!" he shrieked at last.

"It's okay, man," I said, putting a hand on his shoulder. "You don't have to lie about that stuff anymore."

"I'm not lying," he said, his voice almost a sob. "Clear belt!"

"There's no such thing."

"Yes there is. I—I—I did the final test."

"You head-butted a rock in half?"

"Is that what I said I did?" asked Beefer, licking his lips, eyes darting around nervously.

"Yeah."

"Then I *did* head-butt a rock in half!"

"Seriously, you don't have to—"

"I did, and I'll prove it!" said Beefer, and he held the trophy at arm's length in both hands. "Everybody watch *this*!" And he head-butted the marble trophy as hard as he could. It made a painful thudding sound.

"See?" said Beefer with a smug grin on his face. He held up the trophy. Sure enough, there was now a large crack down the middle—it had been broken in half. "Clear b—" But before Beefer could finish the thought, he slumped to the ground, unconscious.

CHAPTER 22

BEEFER WOKE UP a minute or two later. Soon after that a soot-covered Principal Truitt escorted him to the nurse's office for medical attention—but not before we could recover the PETCATRAZ Pro™ key he'd stolen from Mr. Copeland. Luckily, Martha never realized that I had, uh, *borrowed* her key, too.

"Another Little Mister or Miss Muscles trophy destroyed," said Coach Weekes as he held the two broken pieces in his hands. His eyes were moist. "I'm sorry, Sam."

"Eh, it wasn't mine anyway," I said, taking the broken trophy from him. "I cheated during the competition."

Coach Weekes gasped. "Sam, you *what*? How dare you! You desecrated and dishonored a proud and . . . noble . . ." He trailed off, his lip quivering. A big tear rolled down his cheek.

"No need to cry," I said. "I'm really sorry. If you want to give me detention I totally—"

"No!" said Coach Weekes, now blubbering uncontrollably. "I cheated, too! In 1983, I cheated during the Little Mister Muscles competition. I didn't really win! I can't even do a single knuckle-up."

I put a hand on his shoulder as he wailed. "Well, Coach, this year the real winner was Dylan D'Amato." I handed her the two trophy chunks. She beamed.

"Thanks, Sam!" said Dylan. "You can keep the little half for being good at drawing." She handed me back the smaller piece and gave me a big hug. Hamstersaurus Rex grunted as he was squeezed between us.

"You know what this means, don't you, Coach?" said Dylan.

"What?" said Coach Weekes, between heaving sobs.

"We play disc golf in gym class for the rest of the year!" cried Dylan.

"A bet's a bet, D'Amato. Congratulations," he said, sniffling as he shook her hand. "And maybe after class, you could teach me how to do knuckle-ups?"

"Sure, Coach," said Dylan. "It's all about proper form."

"Sam!"

I turned to see Martha Cherie, hands on her hips. "You didn't really follow the proper protocol in all of this," she said.

"You're right," I said. "Guess I'm kind of a maverick."

"In your own strange way, though, I see that you went above and beyond to protect the life of an innocent hamster."

"It was nothing," I said with a shrug.

"No, it was something," said Martha, and she gave me a sudden, awkward hug—which luckily offered a chance to clip the PETCATRAZ Pro™ key back onto her lanyard without her noticing.

"You honored the sacred trust," said Martha. "So by the power vested in me by Horace Hotwater Middle School, I hereby appoint you, Sam Gibbs, to be Junior Deputy Hamster Monitor. . . . Can I do that, Arnold?"

"Sure, whatever," said Mr. Copeland. "But seriously, Martha, it's *Mr. Copeland.* I'm not telling you again."

And so, I accepted my new post as Junior Deputy Hamster Monitor (my own ID and lanyard to come).

Because Science Night had been completely destroyed, the teachers had no choice but to give everyone As. This kept me from learning any valuable lessons about not leaving long-term projects to the very last minute. So that was cool.

All in all, it was a pretty action-packed Tuesday.

"Wow, Science Night sure is *exciting*, huh, Bunnybutt!" said my mom, wiping her nose with a tissue as she returned from the parking lot.

"Yep," I said. "Hey, you're not sneezing anymore."

"Wow. Maybe I'm cured."

She wasn't. I looked down at my pocket. Sure enough—as I'd almost come to expect at this point—Hamstersaurus Rex was gone.

CHAPTER 23

AFTER THE SECOND-CRAZIEST Science Night on record—apparently some kid hypnotized a flock of pigeons to do his bidding two years ago—life at Horace Hotwater Middle School returned to normal.

Martha Cherie raised her hand a lot. Mr. Copeland sighed a lot. Wilbur Weber mentioned snails more than was strictly necessary. Judy, the lunch lady, occasionally took me aside and told me never to give up on my dream of becoming a dancer. I didn't have the heart to tell her I'd been lying.

In gym class, we all worked on our disc golf fundamentals under Dylan's expert guidance.

Coach Weekes even talked about starting an official school team.

There was no more Beefer Vanderkoff, though. Principal Truitt suspended him, and he never returned. Someone told me that he enrolled at L. L. Dupree. In his absence, water fountain fires dropped more than 95 percent. Strange as it may sound, I actually found myself missing the guy once in a while. School can get a little boring without a nemesis bent on your destruction.

I'm not sure what became of Michael Perkins. Rumor had it that long after everyone left Science Night, Roberta Fast did find the snake, hiding under a hatchback in the school parking lot, with the disc golf disc still stuck in his mouth. Supposedly, she took him to SmilesCorp's labs for "special testing." My mom said that was baloney.

There was no Hamstersaurus Rex, either. The PETCATRAZ Pro™ sat empty on a back shelf in Mr. Copeland's classroom, its door swinging open on its hinges.

Pretty soon, most of the other kids seemed to forget about the little guy. Not Martha Cherie, though. Dylan didn't forget Hamstersaurus Rex, either. Grudgingly, the two of them looked for him every day after class, together, just like I had done.

As for me, I kept my Junior Deputy Hamster Monitor ID lanyard—and the brand-new PETCATRAZ Pro™ key Martha had given me—inside my pocket. I missed the little guy, too, but I didn't go searching for him. Instead, I drew pictures. They chronicled the epic saga of a four-ounce mutant folk hero named Hamstersaurus Rex. I drew the falling solar system, Raisin stuck in the filing cabinet, the Sixty-Foot Sandbag Drag, the Antique Doll Museum rampage, and more.

Somehow I knew that wherever he was, whatever he was doing, Hamstersaurus Rex was going to be okay.

And then one day, when we returned to school after Thanksgiving, we all heard a familiar sound from the back of the classroom. It was a growl.

We turned to see Hamstersaurus Rex— stumpy arms waving, tail whipping, beady eyes blinking—sitting inside his cage like nothing had happened.

"Well, kids," said Mr. Copeland with smile. "I guess we have a hamster again."

I approached the cage. Hamstersaurus Rex gave me a toothy grin and a burp of friendship. I laughed and poked my index finger between the bars to give him the world's smallest high five.

TOM O'DONNELL is the author of *Space Rocks!* and its sequel, *Space Rocks! 2: For the Love of Gelo!* He has written for the *New Yorker*, *McSweeney's*, and the television shows *TripTank* and *Billy on the Street*. He lives with his wife in Brooklyn, New York. Read more about him at www.tomisokay.com.

TIM MILLER is an author and illustrator of picture books. He studied at the School of Visual Arts, where he earned his BFA in cartooning. His first picture book, *Snappsy the Alligator (Did Not Ask to Be in This Book)*, received four starred reviews. *Publishers Weekly* called his illustrations "bold and goofy." He lives in Queens, in New York City. You can see more of his work at www.timmillerillustration.com.